Cha... ...ess LLC

ChangelingPress.com

Forge/Casper Duet

Harley Wylde

Forge/Casper Duet
Harley Wylde

All rights reserved.
Copyright ©2022 Harley Wylde

ISBN: 978-1-60521-845-8

Publisher:
Changeling Press LLC
315 N. Centre St.
Martinsburg, WV 25404
ChangelingPress.com

Printed in the U.S.A.

Editor: Crystal Esau
Cover Artist: Bryan Keller

The individual stories in this anthology have been previously released in E-Book format.

Table of Contents

Forge (Reckless Kings MC 4)
Harley Wylde

Whisper -- Abducted at a young age, I'd learned to live with the brutal man who'd kidnapped me. Quick with his fists, he made sure I knew to keep quiet and do as I was told. Until nearly a decade later. When Forge came to confront the man I'm forced to call "Dad," I knew it was my one chance. Saying my true name for the first time was both thrilling and scary. Going to live with a bunch of bikers was even more so. But I found out soon enough there wasn't anything Forge wouldn't do for me. I might have had a crush on him. Just a bit. Then my world imploded once more, and I ran. Now he's back, and I'm terrified and excited all at once.

Forge -- One of the boys who attacked Whisper is out on parole, and I know she's clueless. I only intended to make sure she was all right. How the hell I ended up claiming her son as my own, then marrying her, is beyond me. Can't say I'm too broken up about it. Whisper is all grown up, and I'd be lying if I said I didn't want her.

With her attacker's whereabouts unknown, and my club pissed at me, there's a lot on my plate. But I have to say, bringing Whisper and little Jacob home with me had to be the best idea I ever had. Now that they're mine, I'll do anything to hold onto them.

Prologue

Whisper
Ten Years Ago

I'd tried to stay as small as possible. If they knew I was here, there would be hell to pay. I didn't think I could handle another beating from the man claiming to be my father. It hadn't taken me long to learn to keep my mouth shut when it came to John Gillis. The first time I'd corrected him about my name and who my parents were, I'd received a backhand to my cheek hard enough it had knocked me off my feet. I'd only been seven at the time. It had been the mildest form of punishment I'd received my first year with him. Now I'd grown up enough to know better than to say anything to anger "Dad."

He'd been meeting with a metalsmith about a piece of art, and I'd wanted to see the man who created such beautiful things. I'd seen some of his work, not only around our house, but in town too. They called him Forge, which I'd found to be a funny name. Yet now, seeing him in person, I realized it suited him. He towered over John Gillis, his biceps bulging as he folded his arms over his chest.

"I've already said I'm not interested in doing more work for you," Forge said. "I came because talking to you over the phone doesn't seem to be getting me anywhere. So listen close, asshole. I'm done. I choose my clients, not the other way around, and I'm not going to make you another fucking thing."

John clenched his fists and I wondered if he would be dumb enough to take a swing at the man. Probably not. He tended to only pick on those he deemed weaker than himself. If Forge hit him back, he'd possibly kill him with one blow. Too bad John didn't seem to be brave enough to take the man on. I'd have loved to see him knocked on his ass.

"Not enough money?" John asked.

"It's not about the money. I've heard the rumors around town. I'd prefer not to associate with someone like you."

Shit. That wasn't good. I pressed my fingers to my lips so I wouldn't make a sound. John's face turned purple, and I saw the vein in his temple start to throb. He let loose a roar as he launched himself at Forge.

The big man sidestepped, letting John faceplant on the floor. All my efforts of being quiet fled as I let out a little snicker. My eyes went wide when John glared in my direction. Yeah, he knew I was here now, and the twitch from Forge told me he'd heard me too. I stood, knowing there wasn't any point in trying to hide anymore.

"You little bitch! You think that's funny?" John demanded, advancing on me. It seemed Forge had been forgotten, at least for the moment. Or John had realized he didn't stand a chance against the bigger man.

I took a step away not wanting to let the man get any closer to me. He stomped forward, his arm going back, and I knew it would be bad this time. Worse than before. I flinched, my eyes slamming shut as he came closer. I felt the breeze of his hand coming at my face. And nothing else. I slitted an eye open and gasped when I saw Forge had gripped John's hand, tight enough he'd forced the man to his knees.

"And this is why I won't work with you. Hitting kids makes you a shitty person," Forge said. He glanced at me. "You okay?"

I nodded.

"It's between me and my daughter," John said.

My throat started to close. I'd denied this man as my father long ago, and I'd paid the price. With Forge holding him down, I wondered if I could voice the words again. Someone needed to know who I was, where I'd come from. I didn't want to stay with John Gillis anymore. For that matter, I'd never wanted to live with him. He'd kidnapped me and given me no other options.

"He's not my father," I said, my voice softer than I'd intended. I hadn't been permitted to talk at a normal volume in so long I'd forgotten how.

John tried to break free of Forge's grasp, only to scream like a little girl when the man tightened his hold and twisted. I heard the crack of John's wrist and knew it had been broken. Served him right!

"Who are you?" Forge asked, holding my gaze.

"My name is Willamena Glass, but everyone calls me Whisper. He abducted me when I was seven."

I'd done it! I'd spoken the truth, admitted who I was. It had been so long since I'd even tried. I'd been too scared, too broken by the man now crying like a baby. On my own, I'd have never stood a chance against him. If Forge hadn't come here today, I'd still be silently taking the abuse John heaped on me. Not to mention the horrible things he made me do. My throat tightened again as I thought about all my sins. Would I ever be forgiven? I didn't know if there was a way to atone or not, but I'd try. I didn't want to be a monster like him.

Forge's jaw tightened. "How old are you now?"

"Fifteen."

He scanned me from head to toe. "You don't look fifteen."

It wasn't the first time I'd heard that. It was actually a bonus for John. It made it easier for me to do the job he'd given me. I looked helpless. Then again, I *was* a weak, pathetic little girl who couldn't break free of the likes of John Gillis. I'd often wondered if I'd been bigger, or been a boy, would I have had a chance to escape? Could I have stood up for myself more without getting the beating of a lifetime? Of course, if I'd been a boy, John would have never snatched me off the street. No, he'd wanted a young girl, and I'd been in the wrong place at the wrong time.

"I've always been small. My parents were Mary and Tom Glass from Knoxville, Tennessee. They've probably been searching for me."

Forge pulled out his cell phone, using his other hand as he hadn't released John yet. "Hey, Pres, I need backup over at John Gillis' place. We have a problem."

He ended the call and pocketed his phone. When John tried to stand again, Forge kicked him in the stomach, then kneed him in the face. John passed out, sprawling on the cement floor as Forge finally let go. The show of violence might have scared me once, but after looking evil in the eye every day since I was a kid, I knew how to tell when a man was good and when he had a demon inside. And Forge was one of the good guys. Didn't matter he had a gun tucked at the small of his back, or that he could break bones so easily. He'd protected me from the man who'd hurt me for so long.

I smiled a little. I may not have been able to save myself, but Forge had done it for me. He was a real-life hero! Whatever it took, I'd make sure he knew how appreciative I was, even if it took years to do it. I didn't think a simple thank-you would suffice. I was free! Or at least, I thought I was. Forge wouldn't have hurt John to spare me if he intended bad things, would he? He'd said he didn't like men who hurt kids. Didn't that mean he would not only free me from John Gillis, but help me leave this place? I didn't know how to get home, or if my parents even still lived in the same place.

"What happens now?" I asked.

"My club, the Reckless Kings, will be here in a minute. I'll need you to tell us your story from start to finish, then we'll see if we can get you back to your parents. He hit you often?"

I nodded. "I learned to keep quiet and stay out of his way. It works most of the time, but not always. He's forced me to call him 'Dad' from the beginning."

"He ever touch you sexually?" Forge asked.

My cheeks burned and I shook my head. No, John hadn't snatched me off the street for that purpose. It could have been worse, except I knew what happened to the women he forced me to lure in. It sickened me, and I hated myself for it. Denying him would have resulted in my death, and I'd done what I had to in order to survive.

"He prefers grown women," I said. I eyed the man on the ground. Either he was still out or pretending to be. I didn't trust him.

The sound of motorcycles filled the air and soon four of them pulled up out front. Each man wore the same leather vest as Forge, and I took note of their names. *Brick. Shield. Copper. Snake.* I didn't know how they came up with their names, and in the case of Snake, I wasn't sure I wanted to find out. The wiggly creatures creeped me out. I didn't like things without legs, and I really didn't like ones that had too many, like centipedes.

Forge went to his bike and pulled out a length of rope. He came back and rolled John onto his back, then secured his wrists, binding them tight. When he stood again, he quickly introduced me to the other men, and

I knew my time was up. They'd find out what I'd done. Didn't matter I'd not been given a choice. My actions had caused others to be hurt and had possibly cost them their lives. Bile rose in my throat.

Once they found out, they wouldn't want to help me anymore. Would they hurt me the way Forge had hurt John? I didn't think it would matter I was only fifteen. I'd known what I was doing was wrong. I knew exactly what happened when I defied John Gillis. It didn't matter these men would care.

"He took me off the streets when I was seven. I'd been on my way home from school when a car pulled up to the curb. I'd been warned about talking to strange men and felt nervous when the door closest to me opened. John lunged from the car, wrapped his arm around my waist and put his hand over my mouth as he yanked me into the vehicle. They sped off and that was the last day I saw my parents."

"Do you know why he took you?" Forge asked.

I felt the blood drain from my face. Now was the time. Would I go to jail? Or did they have something worse planned for me? I didn't know these men. Just because Forge had been nice so far, didn't mean they would be so tolerant after they heard the rest.

"He and his friend kept me with them for a few weeks, traveling around the southern part of the country. They..." My hands trembled as I pushed my hair behind my ear. "They made me pretend to need help. When a young woman would offer to get me home, they'd be waiting and abduct her."

I shut my eyes, still hearing their screams and pleas for mercy. A tear slipped down my cheek and I hastily wiped it away. I didn't get to cry. It was my fault those women had suffered. My tears were useless, and offensive to their memory. Those women wouldn't have been hurt if it weren't for me. I didn't think John and his friend would have been able to take them as easily.

I felt a set of strong, solid arms fold around me, and I looked up at Forge. I couldn't remember the last time someone had shown me any sort of comfort or affection. I melted against him and cried until my throat hurt and I didn't think I had any tears left. I'd thought for sure he'd turn his back on me, that these men would want to hurt me after they knew everything. Having him accept me, to not blame me for what I'd done, it meant everything.

"Do you know what they did with the women?" Brick asked. His tone was soft, almost as if he were afraid he'd startle me if he spoke louder.

"They tortured them. Raped them. I didn't know that last part at first or didn't understand. Not until I got older. John made me watch once, when I was eleven. The woman begged and pleaded. I think he did the same to the others, before Gary left." I clenched my eyes shut tight again before opening them. I'd face whatever punishment I got. The time for hiding was over. "I think they may have murdered them after, but I don't know for sure. A few days would pass, and I'd have to do it again."

"You said that lasted a few weeks. What happened after?" Snake asked.

"John and the other man, Gary, had a falling out. I didn't see him after that. John loaded me into the car a few hours after I heard them arguing and we eventually ended up here. He forced me to say I was his daughter, Whisper Gillis. He enrolled me in a homeschool program so people wouldn't ask too many questions." He'd especially not wanted anyone to see the marks he left on me every time he got angry. If he'd sent me to a real school, someone might have seen the bruises, or noticed when I limped or had to hold my ribs when I moved. The last thing John Gillis had wanted was any sort of official person poking their nose into his business.

The one called Shield came closer. "How did he do that? You wouldn't have had any documents. Birth certificate. Shot records. None of that."

I shrugged. "I don't know. I saw a birth certificate once. Not up close, but I did see it had the name Whisper Gillis on it. I guess he had someone make one. I know I wasn't in school the first month he had me. Maybe longer. Is that something he could do easily? I know on TV people get forged documents all the time. I have no idea how hard it would be in real life."

"You're going to come to the clubhouse with us and I'm going to check into your story. I'm going to need any details you remember of your past life. If you're telling the truth, we'll get you home to your family," Shield said.

I didn't like the *if* he'd included. I didn't have anything to hide. I'd told them the truth, but what if they couldn't find anything to prove I wasn't lying? Would they kill me? Turn me over to the cops? What if they believed I really was the daughter of John Gillis? What happened to the kids of murderers and rapists? It would probably be even worse for me since I'd been forced to help him.

"She's a kid, asshole," Brick muttered. "Quit scaring her. Even if she is John Gillis' biological child, it isn't like she could have fought him. Look at her! She's barely a hundred pounds soaking wet. She didn't stand a chance against him."

"I tried," I said. "I refused to say I was his

daughter and he beat me. I've tried to be good since then. Sometimes I still speak out or don't do something the way he wants."

I lifted my shirt and showed them the fist-sized bruises on my torso. As scary as these men were, I needed them to know I hadn't done anything willingly. Taking a breath to steel my nerves, I turned and lowered my leggings over my ass, showing them the marks John had left the other day. It still hurt to sit.

"Motherfucker." I jolted when I heard something smash and turned to see Forge had thrown a glass against the wall. His chest heaved, and he had his eyes shut, a look of agony on his face.

"Keep your clothes on, sweetheart," Brick said softly. "We'll keep you safe until we figure out where you belong."

I nodded, putting my clothes back in place, and tried to hunch my shoulders. Forge came over and pulled me against his chest again, his hand smoothing up and down my back. I clung to him, savoring the contact.

"I'll have a Prospect come pick up John. Whisper can ride with me back to the compound," Forge said. "Someone make sure the clubhouse is cleared out. She doesn't need to see the shit that goes on in there. I want every fucking whore gone by the time I walk through the doors with her."

Whore? Did these men deal in women? Had I only traded one monster for another? I glanced at Forge's face. No. He might have called someone, or several someones a whore, but he hadn't meant in the paid-for-sex kind of way.

"On it," Copper said. He pulled out his phone and stepped away.

Forge took my hand and led me out to his

motorcycle. He paused long enough to send a text message, then swung his leg over the seat of his bike. He started the engine and motioned for me to get on the back. I straddled the bike and looked down, wondering where I should put my feet or my hands. Forge seemed to understand my dilemma and tapped my foot, then pointed out a peg on either side. He gripped my hands and tugged them around his waist.

The ride to their clubhouse was exhilarating! I didn't even care that every bump made me hurt more, even though I'd likely pay the price when we got to our destination, and I got off the motorcycle. I loved the wind in my hair and the feeling of freedom as we zipped through the streets of town and then down a long country road that ended up being their driveway. The building we stopped in front of was beautiful in a rustic way. A line of motorcycles sat out front. Forge pulled up between two and turned off the engine. I tried to stand and nearly landed on my ass when my legs wouldn't hold me.

He smirked and grabbed my waist, holding me up. "Sorry, little girl. Should have warned you."

"I'll be okay."

He got off the bike and took my hand, leading me into the building. I looked around, trying to take it all in. A balcony overlooked the main area and I saw rooms upstairs. A bar ran the length of one wall with mirrors behind it, and lots of alcohol. We kept going, and he pushed open a set of doors that led to what looked like a community room or something. I saw a large table surrounded by chairs, and the emblem from the back of their vests dominated one wall.

Several men sat around the table. Forge stopped next to one of them and pulled out a chair. "Have a seat, baby. I'll stand for now."

He didn't have to tell me twice! My knees gave out as I sank onto the chair. The guy next to me had *Vice President -- Hawk* on his vest. The other man's said *President -- Beast*.

"This is Whisper. Once the others get here, and Shield brings his laptop, we're going to see if we can dig into her past a bit," Forge said.

The man on the other side of the table snorted. I eyed his vest. *Treasurer -- Prospero*. I didn't know what he found funny about the situation.

By the time everyone else came in and took a seat, and Shield had his laptop, I felt like a bug under a microscope. The way everyone watched me made me antsy. I was almost scared to even breathe.

"All right. Tell them everything and go slow so Shield can try and find information to confirm your story as you go," Forge said.

I spilled it all, from beginning to end, and felt both relieved and like I wanted to run away. I saw judgmental gazes from a few of the men, but most looked at me in sympathy. At least I wasn't guilty to everyone at the table. It could have been worse. It seemed Forge believed me at the very least. Otherwise, he wouldn't have gone to so much trouble, right?

Shield winced and looked at Forge. "It's not good. You sure you want me to tell her this shit?"

Forge nodded. "She needs the truth."

"All right." Shield sighed. "Your parents died in a car accident two years ago. They were on their way back from a family vacation."

"Family vacation?" My brow furrowed. "I was an only child. Is it still a family vacation if it's just the two of them?"

"Um." Shield cleared his throat and wouldn't look at me still. "Two years after you disappeared, they had another child. Your brother is six and he's still alive. The accident caused brain damage and he's in a permanent care facility, funded by the state."

They replaced me? After two years, they'd decided to have another baby? Had they even looked for me? Why had they given up on ever seeing me again? The room spun a little and I gripped the edge of the table. I felt a hand land on my shoulder and Forge's scent calmed my racing heart.

"How long?" I asked. "How long until they stopped looking?"

"They reported you missing to the police, searched for about six months, then it seems things went quiet. There was a reward for your safe return. Looks like your mom went to counseling for the first year." Shield tapped on his laptop keys some more. "You have an aunt and uncle in Nashville. Simone and Willis Hughes."

"Mom's brother," I murmured. "I never met them. My parents said they weren't good people."

Shield muttered something that I didn't catch. If he could find all that about me and my parents, then he probably had an idea of why I'd always been told my uncle was a bad person. I didn't think he was as evil as John Gillis had been, but it didn't mean the man was a good guy either. Despite the shades of gray in the world, I'd learned most people fell into one category or the other.

"Looks like you have a choice to make," Beast said. "We can take you to your aunt and uncle, or let the police place you in foster care if your family doesn't want you."

I stared at the table, wishing for another option. I didn't want to live with strangers, but it seemed I didn't have anywhere else to go. No matter what I chose, I'd be with someone I didn't know. I'd heard the horror stories about foster care, but I knew my mom wouldn't have avoided her brother without a good reason.

"It doesn't matter," I said. "I survived this long with John Gillis. I can handle whatever else gets dumped in my lap."

"She's suffered enough, hasn't she? Why not let the girl decide where she wants to live?" Copper said.

"Or there's option three," one of the men said. "One of us could adopt her, or we could see if any other clubs would want to take her in."

"Excellent suggestion, Crow," Beast said. "Anyone want a daughter?"

I felt like either a puppy at the pound, or a piece of art being auctioned off. My gaze scanned the men at the table, and I noticed the one called Brick giving me a thoughtful look. After a moment, he thumped his fist on the table.

"If there's no objections, I'll take her," Brick said. "I'm starting to think I'll never have a woman and kids. Long as she doesn't mind living with a bachelor."

Beast faced me. "Well? What do you want to do, Whisper?"

Decisions, decisions. An aunt and uncle I'd never met, strangers in foster care, or the biker who'd at least been kind so far. I wasn't stupid. Better the devil you knew than the one you didn't.

"I'll stay with Brick."

"Want me to make you his legally adopted daughter?" Shield asked. "Wouldn't take me long."

I didn't know exactly what he meant, but I gave a nod. If I was going to do this, might as well go all in. It wasn't like I had anything to lose.

I held Brick's gaze and saw him smile a little. At

least he seemed happy about this turn of events. I couldn't help but think I'd made the right choice. If my aunt and uncle were fit people to be parents, wouldn't they have custody of the little brother I'd never met? I didn't know if he was in that care facility because it was best for him physically, or because there wasn't anyone else worthy of taking care of him.

As much as I wanted to ask more about him, I couldn't help but feel hurt. Not once in the seven years I'd spent with my parents had they ever mentioned wanting another baby. Had they always wanted more children and hadn't been able to for some reason? Or had I been right and they'd tried to replace me? I wished I could ask them, but I'd never see them again.

John Gillis had taken more from me than I'd realized. Now I didn't even have the chance of ever seeing my family again. They were gone and weren't coming back.

Chapter One

Whisper
Seven Years Ago

"Dad! I'm going to be late. Would you hurry the hell up?" I yelled across the house.

"Where's the fucking fire?" he demanded, stomping into the room in jeans with a blue button-down. He'd put his cut on over it. It was the closest he'd ever get to dressing up and I smiled, thinking he looked nice.

"The fire is called graduation. I need to be there in fifteen minutes or I can't walk. You're the one who made a big deal about me attending the local high school and having a normal life. Guess what? Normal kids walk across the stage and get a diploma, or so I've been told."

"You driving there?" he asked.

"No." I rubbed the toe of my boot on the floor. "I'm getting a ride from a friend."

He froze, his jaw tensing and his eyes narrowing. "Friend? Whisper Evans, I know damn well your friends don't come here to pick you up. Who the hell do you think you're riding with?"

"Tommy Aikens asked to drive me to graduation and to the field party after. He's meeting me at the gate in five minutes. I thought you could give me a ride up there."

He folded his arms and glowered. Brick, otherwise known as Hank Evans, and my adopted father, got that stubborn look in his eyes I knew didn't bode well for me. The day he'd brought me home with him, I'd not known what to expect. I'd once asked what happened to John Gillis, and he'd told me the man had been taken care of. I'd not asked again.

Something told me they hadn't handed him over to the police.

After I'd come to live with Brick, it had taken us a week to settle into a routine and get to know one another. Now it felt like I'd been his daughter all my life. I couldn't imagine anyone I'd rather have for a dad. He'd been amazing, and he didn't even give me shit about my crush on Forge.

I fingered the necklace I never took off. It had started as a piece of his artwork but had broken off. I'd commented on how pretty it was, so he'd smoothed out the edges, drilled a hole through it, and put it on a chain for me. Sadly, the big guy had only ever seen me as a child, and probably always would.

"Come on, Dad! I'm leaving for college in three days. Let me have a little fun tonight."

He sighed and ran a hand through his hair. "Fine. But don't come home pregnant or I'll have to kill a motherfucker."

I threw my arms around him and hugged him tight. "Thanks, Dad. I promise I won't stay out too late."

"Come on. I'll drop you at the gate and then ride out with the others. You wait *inside* the fence. You hear me? Lyle is on duty, and he'll let you out when your *friend* gets here."

I rolled my eyes. "We really are just friends, Dad. You know I don't date. Never have, don't plan to start now."

Well, not entirely true. If a certain foxy older man ever looked at me as more than a kid, then I'd jump at the chance to date. Forge had saved me the day he'd come to meet with John Gillis, and I'd had a bit of hero worship going on. Then I'd started spending time with him and fell head over heels. No boy could ever measure up.

I followed Dad outside and got on the back of his bike, tucking my dress under my thighs so it wouldn't blow in the wind and give everyone a show. When we got to the front of the compound, he dropped me off and I waited with Lyle. The guy was sweet and a bit goofy with me, even though I'd also seen him covered in blood after gutting someone. I'd noticed a lot of the men here showed me a side they hid from most people. It made me feel special.

I bounced on my toes when I saw Tommy's truck coming down the lane. I poked Lyle in the ribs until he opened the gate and I rushed out to meet the boy most girls swooned over. Every girl except me. Tommy was good-looking, and knew it, but he didn't have any of the qualities I admired in a guy. Not to mention, he was too young.

I hopped into the truck, and he reached over for a hug. I awkwardly patted his shoulder and pulled away as quick as I could. It didn't take long to reach the school, and the whirlwind of graduation started. My heart raced as I thought about the future. I'd agreed to attend school in state, but Dad had compromised on a college farther away than Nashville.

By the time I walked across the stage, it felt like butterflies were swooping around in my stomach. I heard my dad and the Reckless Kings screaming and cheering as I accepted my diploma. Cheeks on fire, I scanned the audience and waved, spotting Forge sitting right next to my dad. The rest of the ceremony passed in a blur and soon it was over.

Dad found me in the crowd and hugged me tight. "So proud of you, Whisper."

"Thanks, Dad."

I also got a hug from Beast, Hawk, Crow, Shield,

and Forge. If I held onto him a little longer than the others, no one said anything. I'd have held on and never let go if I thought it wouldn't freak Forge out. He'd never given any indication he saw me the same way I did him. He starred in my every fantasy.

"We'll have a celebration breakfast in the morning with everyone and you'll get your gifts then," Dad said. "Don't stay out too late."

"Where's she going?" Forge asked, his brow furrowed as he looked at my dad.

"Field party," I said. "The entire class is going."

Slight exaggeration, but they didn't need to know that. Other than myself and Tommy, I knew of at least a dozen other students going to the field party. With a graduating class of one hundred ten students, I'd guess that less than a quarter would show up. Most had plans with family.

"Be safe, and if that Tommy guy drinks too much and you need a ride home, you give me a call," Dad said.

"And if you can't reach him, you call me." Forge reached over and tugged my hair. "You hear me?"

I nodded. "Got it. Call Dad or you if I need a way home. I'll be fine. Promise."

I walked off to find Tommy. I should have known he'd be smoking away from all the adults. He put out the cigarette as I got closer and gave me what he probably thought was a panty-dropping smile. Unfortunately for Tommy, it didn't do anything for me. His friend, Chris, stood a few feet away with a girl I'd never spoken to before. I knew her name, but not much else about her.

"You ready for some fun?" Tommy asked.

"Yep! Let's go celebrate our freedom!" I grinned. "May we enjoy it while it lasts because I've heard college will be twice as hard with tons more work."

We piled into Tommy's truck and drove to the field behind an old, abandoned barn. It's where the kids hung out on weekends when the weather cooled off. Two metal barrels stood ten feet apart and I knew a fire would be going soon. Not that we needed the heat! Far from it. Tennessee in May wasn't exactly cold. In another month, it would feel like my face was melting off whenever I went outside.

Tommy and Chris started a fire in each barrel. Other vehicles arrived, and with them came coolers of soda, water, and beer. Someone set out two cardboard boxes full of snack cakes and chips. I grabbed some chips and a bottle of water. If I wanted to drink, I knew I needed to do it at the compound, where I'd be safe. Dad had drilled it into my head to never accept an open container from anyone, never leave my drink unattended, and to definitely not drink alcohol unless I knew with absolute certainty I wouldn't get hurt.

I sipped my water and listened to the conversations around me. Tommy moved closer and slung his arm over my shoulders. As much as I wanted to pull away, I didn't want to make it obvious and hurt his feelings, or his pride. I knew he had a reputation around school. Why he'd wanted to attend the party with me I'd never understand. I'd made sure he knew we could only ever be friends, and he seemed cool with it.

Someone cranked the radio in their car, leaving the engine running and the headlights on so we wouldn't be in complete darkness. A few couples started dancing and Tommy grabbed my water, setting it aside, to pull me into the small crowd forming. I laughed as we danced, the music thumping hard enough I felt the vibrations through the ground.

"Having a good time?" Tommy asked.

I nodded and let him lead me back over to his friends. The girl who'd come with Chris handed my water bottle back to me. I hesitated to drink it. Brick and Forge had always insisted if I went to any parties to never accept an open container. Despite my past, I didn't think another girl would do anything to hurt me. These were high school students, not pervy old men. It wasn't like the girl had a grudge against me.

I chugged the remaining water, wanting to hydrate. Sweat already coated my skin and made my clothes cling to me. After a few minutes, I started to sweat more, and my vision began to blur. I swayed as I blinked, trying to stay awake. My limbs felt heavy and soon I listed to the side. I heard Tommy laugh as he held me close. What the hell was wrong with me?

I either passed out, or was so high on whatever I'd been given, I completely spaced out for a while. Long enough the party had ended, and reality started to seep back in. The air had cooled, all the lights were gone, including the fires, and I realized I was alone in the field. I struggled to sit up, only to lean over and vomit. I cried as I heaved again, emptying the contents of my stomach.

When I'd finished, I wiped the back of my hand across my mouth and patted my clothes, looking for my phone. I froze when I realized something was incredibly wrong. My vision hadn't fully cleared yet, but I could see enough to realize the top of my dress had been ripped and someone had cut my bra.

"No," I murmured. "No, no, no. This isn't happening."

I cried as I struggled to find my phone, finally locating it a few feet away in the grass. My hands shook. I wanted my dad, but I was too scared to call him. Or anyone else. I couldn't stay out here all night, though. I found his name in my contacts and tapped the screen to call him.

"Did that no good motherfucker drink too much?" he asked the second the call connected.

"Daddy." My voice broke and I started sobbing so hard I couldn't breathe.

The line was quiet, but I knew he was still there. "Don't move, Whisper. I'm on my way."

Time had no meaning as I waited. Soon I heard the loud V8 engine of one of the club trucks pull up. The lights hit my face and I held my hand up to shield my eyes. The door opened and I heard someone running to me. No. More than one.

"Jesus," Dad murmured. "I'm going to kill that fucking kid."

I heard a rustle of fabric, and someone pulled a T-shirt over my head. By the scent, I knew it belonged to Forge. Knowing he was here, seeing me like this, only made me cry harder.

"Daddy. I don't feel good," I said. I'd barely uttered the words before I threw up again.

"Find him," Dad said, his voice a low growl. "I want the asshole responsible, and I want him right the fuck now."

Rough fingers smoothed my hair back from my face and I realized it was Forge. I leaned into his touch, whimpering a little.

"Where's it hurt, angel?" Forge asked.

My cheeks burned and I turned my face away, not wanting to talk about it. Not to him or anyone else I looked up to. I'd been so stupid. I'd known not to drink the water after I'd left it. Yet I trusted it was okay because a girl had handed it to me. Had the boys used her the way John Gillis had used me? Or had the girl been just as rotten and evil as the boys who'd done this to me?

"She needs a hospital," Crow said, his voice soft and low. Had my dad brought everyone with him? I looked at the men surrounding me and realized it was just the three of them.

My phone started going off with non-stop notifications. Dad scrolled through it and let loose with a roar loud enough to do a bear proud. Forge took the phone and scrolled through it. The look in his eyes turned darker with every passing second.

"What is it?" I asked.

"If those fuckers were that stupid, I say let the law have them," Crow said. "Not like we can't make sure their time in prison isn't memorable. Or fatal. They need to suffer."

"Do it," my dad said. "I'm taking her to see a doctor. Have someone pick you up from the ER. I don't want to take the time to drop you off at the clubhouse."

Crow took my phone from Forge and started sending himself screenshots, then gave the phone back. Dad lifted me into his arms, and I sagged against him. How had the day gone from exciting to a nightmare so fast? From the way my body ached, and the state of my clothes, I knew what Tommy had done to me. I didn't need anyone to tell me. I'd been holding onto my virginity with the stupid idea Forge would one day see me as a woman and not a child. Now it was gone, stolen by an asshole who'd drugged me.

Forge got into the backseat and held his arms out. Dad handed me off to him, and the big guy held me in his lap. I snuggled against his bare chest and tried to hold it together. I'd once told the club I could handle anything after living with John Gillis. I should have never dared the universe in such a way. Now I was paying the price. A thought occurred to me. I looked up at Forge, trying to see his features in the dark.

"Is this payback?" I asked.

His arms tensed. "What?"

"For what I did? All those women. They were raped and probably killed, all because I did what John Gillis told me to do. Is this my punishment?"

He ran his hand down my hair. "No, angel. None of that was your fault, and neither is this. Those boys were stupid enough to film everything."

"Forge! Shut the fuck up," Dad said.

Boys. Plural. I leaned over and threw up in the floor, hoping it didn't get on Forge's boots. My dad cursed some more, and he pressed the accelerator a little harder, the truck rocketing down the street. He skidded to a halt in front of the hospital and Forge got out with me in his arms. He carried me into the ER, where Dad was already barking at people.

A nurse came over, a stern look on her face, until she saw me. Her eyes went wide and her lips parted. "What happened to her?"

Forge handed me to my dad and pulled my phone from his pocket. He turned down the volume so I couldn't hear, then played a video for the nurse. Her face went red, and she started shouting orders. After a few murmured words from Forge, she also demanded the police be called. I didn't know if Forge had requested it, or if it was policy.

Forge cupped my cheek. "We'll be here waiting for you, angel. Tell them whatever you remember. I'll see the police get all the evidence they need to nail those fuckers to the wall. You hear me? You be strong and we'll get through this."

We. He'd said *we'll* get through this. I gave him a

nod and my dad carried me through the doors and followed the nurse to a curtained-off area. The rest of the night was spent having tests run, taking the morning-after pill, and answering non-stop questions. During the rape exam, my dad stepped outside the curtain, but remained close enough I could hear his voice. Knowing he remained nearby set me at ease.

It took forever before I was released, after being treated for possible STDs and then given another pill to prevent pregnancy. When we got home, Dad carried me straight to my bathroom and set me down. He started the shower, getting the water steaming hot, then laid out clean pajamas for me. He cupped my cheek and kissed my forehead.

"I'm so fucking sorry, Whisper. I'll make sure they pay for what they did to you. If the police won't handle it, I'll take matters into my own hands. You want me to wait outside the door?"

I nodded, tears burning my throat and eyes as I held them back. I showered until the water ran cold, scrubbing my skin raw. Even though I was beyond tired, I didn't think I'd be able to sleep. Dad put me to bed, pulled the covers over me, then lay on top of them. Close enough I could feel the heat of his body, but far enough apart we didn't touch.

"I'll be here all night," he said. "I'm not leaving you."

"Thank you, Daddy." I shut my eyes and felt the tears slip down my cheeks. "I love you."

"Love you too, Whisper. We'll get through this, all right? Whatever you need, you'll have it."

I reached over and found his hand, lacing our fingers together. I knew the club would stand by my side through whatever was heading my way. I just didn't realize exactly how much my life would change.

Chapter Two

Forge
Present Day

I sat on my bike in the shadows, watching her like a damn stalker. I'd never met anyone stronger than Whisper Evans. She took the hand of the little boy at her side and smiled down at him. My gut clenched. We'd been told the morning-after pill didn't always work, and it seemed it had failed our girl. Not that she'd uttered a word of complaint.

She'd left for college a few days later than planned and had returned for the trial. Her rapists were behind bars, and the girl they'd forced to help them had gotten probation. The club made sure the boys received a warm welcome once they were locked up. Each boy had been the bitch of multiple men inside. We kept close tabs on them, making sure they didn't die, no matter how much they wanted to. We'd made sure they suffered, until they'd been granted parole. Two hadn't made it out of the prison, but one did... and that motherfucker was the reason I'd taken to keeping an eye on Whisper and little Jacob.

As far as the club was concerned, Whisper had never existed. Brick had insisted. It hadn't made any fucking sense to me, and I'd argued adamantly. In the end, I'd lost. Whisper had wanted to start her life over, away from the town where all her nightmares had come true. I couldn't blame her. I just didn't understand why we had to pretend she'd never lived at the compound or been part of our lives. The others might be able to walk away, but I couldn't.

I knew Brick came to see his daughter and grandson once a month. He hadn't fooled me. I'd known exactly where he went for each of his road trips, when he claimed he needed time to himself. I'd asked Shield to track him once, then visited the address later on my own. I'd stuck to the shadows, like now, and felt like my heart had been ripped out when I saw a very pregnant Whisper walk out to her car. She'd trusted us to protect her, and we'd failed. *I* had failed. That sweet girl had been my constant companion for years. Having her ripped away made it feel like I'd lost part of myself. Didn't help I'd started to notice little Whisper was all grown up. If only I'd said or done something different before that night. Could I have stopped her from attending the field party?

After that day, I'd done what I could to try and make it up to her. She never saw me, never knew I watched over her, but I did. From a distance. I'd also taken it upon myself to check on the little brother she'd never known. I'd gone to visit him a few times, until the last visit. A nurse had greeted me and given me the sad news that little Maxwell Glass had passed away. Although, it was honestly a blessing. Kid wasn't really living. Far as I knew, no one else in the club knew about Whisper's brother. If Brick had ever checked on the kid, he'd never said anything.

Would Whisper want to know?

She stopped at a park and let Jacob play for a bit. The way she looked around every now and then told me she sensed my presence, or at least realized someone was watching her. As much as I didn't want to freak her out, I wasn't sure she'd exactly welcome me with open arms either. I'd seen her at what she thought was her worst. Even now, remembering that night, made me want to beat someone senseless. Finding her like that had nearly destroyed me.

I walked my bike a little closer, studying the woman she'd become. She'd cut her hair so it fell just past her shoulders. The shorts she wore cupped her ass and fell to mid-thigh. Her shirt might be a loose lavender tee, but it only made me wonder what she looked like underneath it. She'd been beautiful when she was eighteen, and now I found her even more so.

She looked around again until her gaze landed on me. Only the front wheel of my bike could be fully seen from my location, and yet she seemed to relax the moment she spotted my hiding place. She called to her son, and they approached at a sedate pace. The tension had eased from her shoulders and a slight smile curved her lips when she got closer.

"You following me, Forge?" she asked.

God, when had I last heard her voice? "Hey, Whisper."

Jacob cocked his head to the side and studied me. My size and ink didn't seem to scare him, neither did my cut. Then again, he might recognize his grandfather's colors. I'd imagine Brick had taught him about the Reckless Kings at some point, even if we weren't supposed to contact Whisper. Didn't mean his mom and grandfather had kept him in the dark about the club.

"Are you my dad?" Jacob asked.

Whisper's eyes went wide, and I stared at the small boy. Hell, not all that small. Kid had to be little more than six years old now, and yet he nearly came up to his mom's shoulder. I'd bet money on him clearing six feet by middle school, just like I had. Brick was about to be pissed at me, and possibly Whisper too, but as Jacob watched me, I knew exactly what I was going to do. No kid should ever hear their dad was a piece of shit rapist, and I'd be damned if I'd ever let Jacob know about the man who fathered him. Assuming Whisper even knew which one it was.

I glanced at his mom before locking eyes with him again. "Yeah, Jacob. I'm your dad."

I heard Whisper's sharp inhale and when I looked at her again, I saw tears in her eyes. She rapidly blinked to hold them back and bit down on her bottom lip. The *thank-you* she mouthed to me had me getting off the bike and kneeling in front of the boy I'd just claimed as my own. Why I hadn't thought to do it sooner I didn't know. Kid had to have wondered about his father for at least the last year or two. Maybe longer. I didn't know what age kids started to notice things like different homes had two parents while some only had one.

Sure, I'd kept my distance. But I'd been watching over the two of them since before Jacob was born. What would it have hurt to let Whisper see me before now? I could have claimed Jacob as my son and visited once a month or more. Boy needed men in his life. I knew he had Brick, but had it been enough? Then again, I'm not sure me dropping by every now and then would have been much better. Might have only made things worse.

"Why haven't you come here before now?" Jacob asked.

"It's not always easy for me to get away. I have a lot of responsibilities." I reached out and ran my fingers through his hair, noting it was similar in color to mine. Close enough he really could pass for my son. "But I'm here now. For at least tonight. I need to head home in the morning."

Jacob looked up at Whisper. "Can we hang out with Dad until he has to leave?"

The kid wasn't asking nearly as many questions as I'd have expected. It made me wonder what Whisper had said to him so far. Shouldn't he be either overly excited, or really pissed at me? He almost seemed emotionless about the entire thing. I didn't have a ton of experience with kids, but something felt off about all this. Yep, I should have let Whisper know I was hanging around before now. At least, for Jacob's sake. I wondered if his easy acceptance had more to do with him being starved for a father's love and attention than anything else.

I watched Whisper and noticed she seemed a little pale. I didn't know if it was my presence, or the fact her son wanted to spend time with me. Did she think I'd tell the kid I was his father, then run first chance I had? I knew we hadn't been around each other in a long while, but did she really see me as a big enough asshole to do something like that? "I'm fine with it as long as your mom is."

"Were you going to tell me you were here?" she asked.

I could lie. It didn't sit well with me to do so, though. I shook my head. "I've been given orders to keep my distance. I only stopped by to check on you."

She wrapped her arms around her middle. "This isn't the first time, is it?"

"No, it's not. I've known where you are for a while. I drive out every few weeks just to make sure you're all right. Both of you."

Jacob tipped his chin up. "Who said you can't see us? Was it Grandpa?"

Shit. I'd forgotten there were little ears listening, and the boy apparently had excellent hearing. I bit the inside of my cheek. I wasn't about to toss Brick under the bus. Not when he'd been the only male role model in Jacob's life. "The President of my club. He thought it would be best if I didn't see you or your mom."

Fuck. Beast was going to kill me if that got back

to him. Hell, he might do it anyway because I'd not only been checking on Whisper, but I'd gotten caught. And now I'd told the boy I was his father. Yeah, I wouldn't be digging myself out of this hole anytime soon. Did I regret it? Not even a little. The way Jacob looked at me only made me wish I'd broken the rules a lot sooner.

"Is there somewhere we can talk?" I asked Whisper. I hadn't intended to tell her one of the boys who'd raped her had been released, but I didn't know if the prison would call her. They were supposed to. I also knew there was a big difference in should and would. Just because it was protocol for someone to notify her, didn't mean it would happen.

"Can I show Dad my room?" Jacob asked.

It felt like I'd been kicked in the chest by a damn mule every time the kid referred to me as his father. I might have claimed the title, but hearing someone call me Dad? Hell, it filled a need I hadn't even realized I'd had. What if I'd come for Whisper sooner? Could I have convinced her to let me be part of Jacob's life from the beginning?

"You want to follow us?" Whisper asked. "It's just down the street and around the corner."

"I know." I smiled. "I'll meet you there."

She led Jacob away. I watched until they reached the end of the block, then started my bike and followed. The little house she rented had a homey feel to it. The pale blue exterior seemed cheery with a plethora of flowers adding more color. Her car sat in the driveway. The same vehicle she'd had in high school. I'd helped Brick pick it out, and the club had covered the cost. It had been her sixteenth birthday present from all of us. As much as I hated foreign cars, I'd known the Camry would last her a while. It had only been three years old when we'd bought it.

I pulled up behind her car and shut off the engine on my bike. Whisper and Jacob waited at the door, and I followed them into the house. The small two-bedroom, one-bath cottage would have been plain, except Whisper had made it her own. The art on the beige walls stood out with vibrant colors. I recognized the couch and knew Brick had brought it to her. It explained why he'd decided to get a new one. He'd known his daughter needed the old one more than he did. She'd added blue-and-green throw pillows, as well as a multi-colored throw.

All the little touches she'd added made a difference. It wasn't a bad place for a kid to grow up. Jacob had his own room, a yard to play in, and seemed to be a relatively happy child. He hadn't missed any meals, and I had a feeling he was a model student. I didn't see Whisper letting him get away with bad grades or a poor attitude. All my observations showed me what a great mom she was.

"Can I show him my room now?" Jacob asked.

Whisper nodded and I let Jacob take my hand. He tried to drag me down the short hall, making me smile. The kid had a good grip for someone so young. His bedroom had a twin bed, small dresser, a bookshelf filled with what looked to be picture books and early readers, and a chest of toys set against one wall. The framed poster over his bed showed a vintage Harley Davidson, and I noticed a metal Harley on top of his dresser. I picked it up, recognizing it as one of mine.

Anyone could have bought one from the shop. Except I'd have known if Whisper came in. If she'd been anywhere near town, I'd have heard about it, and I'd have made sure I saw her. Then again, if she'd ever come back, I wasn't so sure I'd have let her leave again. I didn't know how Brick let her live here without dragging her home every time he came to visit. He had to miss her. I sure fucking had.

"Where did you get this?" I asked.

"Grandpa gave it to me. He said someone special made it."

My throat felt tight, and I swallowed hard. Shit. I didn't know why Brick would have called me someone special. Jacob had never met me. Unless it was due to Whisper's crush on me when she'd been younger. Or the way I'd always made time for her. At first, it had been cute, having the teenager follow me around. Then she'd gotten older and my feelings had started to change. Too bad I hadn't done something about it sooner.

"He did, huh?"

Jacob nodded. "Do you know who made it?"

"Yeah, buddy, I do." I set it back down and knelt in front of him. "I made it. That's what I do when I'm not busy handling things for the club. I run a metalworks shop. I make things like that motorcycle to sell in a shop the club owns, as well as other pieces of art. I also do some commission pieces."

"Mom said the necklace she wears was made by the same person," Jacob said.

Fuck me. I didn't realize she still wore that little bit of metal around her neck. I hadn't noticed it today, which meant she had it tucked under her shirt, or didn't wear it all the time. My chest ached and I wanted to rub the spot over my heart. His words damn near slayed me. Had Whisper thought about me all this time?

"I gave it to your mom when she was younger. I didn't realize she still had it."

Jacob brushed his toe across the carpet, staring down at the floor. "Did you not want us? Is that why we don't live with you? Didn't you love us even a little?"

Fucking hell. Kid was killing me. When I'd claimed I was his dad, I hadn't thought everything through. If I'd known I'd need to make up an entire story, I might have hesitated to utter those words. Then again, probably not. I couldn't look at his face and destroy his world. He clearly wanted a father in the worst way. I might not be the best guy for the job, but it seemed it was mine now anyway, and I'd do my best to make sure Jacob never regretted being mine.

"Me not being here didn't have anything to do with you or your mom. I didn't know your mom was pregnant when she left for college. She didn't know either. You were a big surprise." That sounded like a reasonable explanation, didn't it? I had no idea how much he knew, if anything.

"The bad kind?" he asked, his voice small.

"No, Jacob. Your mom loves you very much." I reached out and cupped his cheek. "I love you too."

"Jacob, let me talk to your dad for a minute," Whisper said from the doorway. "Why don't you draw him a picture? You can use your new crayons and paper."

Jacob nodded and went to his dresser, pulling open the bottom drawer. I saw it contained a decent amount of art supplies, paper, and coloring books. I went to the kitchen with Whisper and accepted the cup of coffee she handed me.

"I brewed a pot, but maybe I should have found something stronger. Did something happen to Dad? Is that why you're here?" she asked.

I leaned against the counter and stared into my

cup a moment. "No, nothing is wrong with Brick. I didn't mean for you to see me. I just needed to make sure you were safe."

"Why wouldn't I be?" she asked.

"They let him out, Whisper."

I didn't even have to specify who I meant. She knew. Or at least she knew I meant one of her attackers, if not the exact guy. She paled and started shaking her head.

"No. No, no, no. They wouldn't."

I set the mug aside and reached for her, pulling her into my arms. "I'm so sorry, angel. The club took care of two of them, but Tommy got out on parole. He's a free man, and I worried he might come for you. I can't say for sure where he went after his release. He may not know where you are or may not even care. I had to come see for myself that you were okay."

She clutched my shirt and buried her face against my chest. "Why didn't anyone tell me? How long has he been out?"

"Got out yesterday. As to the other, I don't know."

"What do I do now, Forge? I can't just carry on like nothing is wrong. How can I go to work, let Jacob ride the bus home from school, and not worry that monster will wreck my life again?"

"I won't let him get to you, Whisper. I fucked up and didn't protect you before. I won't make the same mistake."

Her hold on me tightened and she lifted her face. "What happened wasn't your fault. Not once have I ever blamed you."

"I know. But I blame myself. For a lot of reasons."

"Name one," she demanded.

I ran my hand up and down her back. "I should have asked you to hang out with the club that night. Maybe if I'd said something, made a big enough deal about it, you'd have passed on the field party."

"What are you saying?" she asked, her hold on me loosening. She took a step back. "Did you... You knew about my crush on you?"

She looked a little horrified, and I was starting to wish I hadn't said anything. It didn't slip my attention she spoke in the past tense, as in she didn't have those same feelings for me anymore. Brick had said she hadn't dated anyone since leaving. I wondered if he'd been telling the truth, or if maybe she did have someone in her life and none of us knew about them. Then again, I hadn't seen her in years. Maybe absence didn't make the heart grow fonder in this case.

I couldn't exactly call back the words. They were spoken and now I'd have to deal with the fallout.

"Yeah. I knew. I was flattered. Still am. Having a girl like you stare at me with stars in your eyes? Hell of an ego boost." I shoved my hands in my pockets. "I had a feeling if I'd asked you stay with me that night, you would have. I'm so fucking sorry, Whisper."

She took a breath and let it out. "All right. There's no point playing the what-if game. It doesn't change anything, and honestly, I love Jacob. I had nightmares about that night for so long, but not once have I ever regretted keeping him."

"Whatever you want me to do, I'll do it. Want me to leave? I'll head out right now." I didn't want to. Hell, if I were being honest, I liked the thought of spending time with Whisper and Jacob. More than that, hearing him call me Dad made me want to hang onto the two of them forever.

She glanced over her shoulder before coming

closer again. "You told Jacob you're his father."

I nodded. Yep. I'd done that. Probably shouldn't have without talking to Whisper first. It seemed I was fucking shit up all over the place today, at least where she was concerned.

"I don't want to stay here alone," she said. "I don't feel safe knowing Tommy is out there somewhere. But I don't know if the club would welcome me back. Dad would let us stay with him. Will Beast give me and Jacob permission? And what happens when he calls you his dad in front of everyone?"

I didn't know what Beast would or wouldn't do these days. Since finding Lyssa and starting a family, he'd been different. We now had three families at the Reckless Kings. Beast, Hawk, and Ranger had all claimed women and had kids. Still, Whisper had made the choice to walk away before, and had Brick ask us to forget she existed. I wasn't sure Beast would be too forgiving, even though she'd had a good reason to leave.

"You don't know, do you?" she asked softly.

I shook my head. "He's got a woman and daughter, with another baby on the way. Hawk and Ranger settled down too. The Reckless Kings are changing in some ways, and still the same in others."

"I betrayed the club by leaving the way I did."

"That's probably how Beast sees it. Won't know unless we call and ask. Do you want me to?"

She rolled her shoulders forward, hunching to make herself small, just like she'd done when I'd first met her. Even then she'd been one of the strongest people I'd met. At seven she'd been kidnapped and had managed to survive while living with a rapist and murderer. Not only that, but she'd done it without completely losing herself.

"Is there any other way?"

"Anything at all?" I asked.

"Yes. I'll do whatever it takes to keep Jacob safe."

I rubbed my hand over my mouth, not sure I should voice my opinion or not. There was one way she might be allowed back. I didn't think she'd like it, though. And I wasn't sure I was ready to head down that road. I might want to protect her, keep her safe, and I'd love nothing more than to kiss the hell out of her, but... some things couldn't be taken back. What I had in mind was one of them.

"Just tell me! Whatever it is, I can handle it," she said. "Even if... if I had to be a... a..."

I narrowed my eyes, having an idea of where she was heading with that one. "A fucking club whore? I swear to Christ, Whisper, if that's what you're trying to spit out, I'm going to spank your ass until you can't sit for a damn week."

She bit her lip and her cheeks flushed as she looked away. Damnit. My cock got hard as I thought about turning her over my knee. Except there was an impressionable little boy not too far away. I wouldn't dare do something like that when he could walk in at any moment.

I stalked closer to her, growling softly at the thought of anyone in the club putting their hands on her. If they even tried to get her to suck them off, or put their cock in her, I'd tear them to shreds. Assuming Brick didn't beat me to it. Why I felt like such a possessive asshole when it came to her, I didn't know. I wasn't going to analyze it too closely.

I cupped her chin and forced her to look at me. "I'm only going to say this once. You want back in? Want the club's protection? There's only one way I can think to do it. And it requires you and me getting a whole lot closer and making me that little boy's dad in a very legal way. You get me?"

She just stared, and I noticed her pulse was pounding.

"County Clerk's office should still be open. Time's ticking, Whisper. You coming home with me? Because if you are, you better get your ass in the car and meet me at the courthouse. We'll get the license, then ask the judge to marry us."

"You'd do that for me? For us?" she asked.

I leaned in closer, my nose nearly brushing hers. "Angel, let's be real clear here. We do this, it's not a sham. It means having you in my bed every fucking night. You get me?"

A shudder racked her small frame, and she gave a slight moan. The way her eyes darkened told me plenty. Seemed that crush was still alive and well, and my little angel wouldn't mind spreading her thighs for me at all. In fact, I wondered if she'd thought about it as often as I had over the last seven years.

Yeah, I'd admit it. I'd jerked one out more than once to thoughts of Whisper. I might have fucked a few club whores or random women over the last seven years, but when it was just me and my hand, it was Whisper I envisioned. Her lips around my cock. Her begging me to fuck her. Shit, I was getting hard just thinking about it. And now there was a chance I'd have the real thing?

"I'll get Jacob," she said.

"Good girl. I'll be waiting outside for you." I kissed her, a quick, hard press of our lips together, then walked out before I was tempted to stay and do far more.

Beast was going to have my ass over this, but

once Whisper was legally mine, there was no turning back. He wouldn't force me out of the club, and there was no damn way I'd live apart from her. Which meant the Reckless Kings would be welcoming her back into the fold, whether they wanted to or not. I knew I should call Brick and give him a heads-up, but I didn't want to chance him getting here in time to stop the wedding.

They'd all find out later.

After it couldn't be undone.

Chapter Three

Whisper

I blinked at the ring on my finger, wondering when Forge had made it. I could tell it wasn't something he'd bought from a jewelry store. At the same time, it didn't look like his work either. But if he'd commissioned it, who had he intended to give it to? I'd not once asked if he'd been seeing anyone. Then again, he hadn't asked me either.

I felt a little sick, imagining him having a girlfriend. Had I just wrecked things for someone else? I didn't think Forge was the type of guy who'd marry me while he had feelings for anyone else, but what if I was wrong? I hadn't seen him in seven years. People changed. He had never been an asshole to me. Was he different with other women?

Jacob had chattered the entire way there and back home. He'd talked through dinner, so excited he could barely sit still. Going from only having a mom to having a dad and finding out we'd be moving closer to his grandpa, had my son bouncing like a rubber ball. I'd been amazed when he'd fallen asleep mid-sentence, leaning against Forge on the couch as they'd watched an animated movie.

"Any regrets yet?" I asked as he tucked Jacob into bed.

Forge came into the hall, pulling Jacob's door shut behind him. "Why? You sorry you agreed to be mine?"

I shook my head and held up my left hand. "Not even a little, but I can't help wondering if the woman who should have had this ring might be a little pissed when we go back. You didn't pick this up on your way to the courthouse. It's custom-made."

He grabbed my hand and led me into the bathroom, shutting and locking the door behind us. "Strip. We're not having this conversation until we're both naked and in the shower. I want to make sure you can't escape."

I snorted at the thought of me ever running from him. Although, I sort of had already. It hadn't been Forge I'd left so much as the painful memory of what I'd suffered. Knowing he'd been one of the ones to find me hadn't helped, but I may have eventually gotten over my embarrassment. Of course, he worried I'd run away. Just what was he going to tell me? Dad hadn't ever mentioned Forge having someone serious in his life. But then Dad also hadn't said anything about Beast, Hawk, and Ranger claiming old ladies either. I had no idea what changes had occurred back home while I'd been gone, and yeah, I still thought of the place as home.

My cheeks heated as I undressed, trying not to stare as Forge began removing his clothes. His broad chest had a smattering of hair across it. The dark strands had started to get a little silver mixed in. Over the years, I'd seen him both clean-shaven and with a short beard. At the moment, his jaw only had a five-o'clock shadow, but I noticed a hint of silver there too in a few spots. The man had aged well. Who was I kidding? I felt myself growing slick just looking at him. I'd never been so turned on in my life, and he hadn't even touched me.

Forge started the water and helped me over the side of the tub before joining me and shutting the curtain. He pressed me against the tiled wall, caging me between his arms. Despite the water still being a little cool, the space felt incredibly hot. Or maybe it was my body reacting to the closeness of the one man

I'd always wanted and thought I'd never have.

"The ring," I reminded him. "Who was it for?"

"Hawk made it for me as payment about a year ago. Said maybe one day I'd have a use for it. I've carried it in my pocket for the last four months."

"Forge, that doesn't..."

He pressed his finger to my lips, silencing me. "I haven't been serious with a woman in over a decade, Whisper. I won't lie and say I've been a monk. There have been women. Never in my house. Just casual hook-ups to let off some steam. I have no idea why Hawk thought I'd ever need that ring, but I'm damn glad I had it."

I swallowed hard, my heart hurting at the thought of him with someone else. "And the last time you had a hook-up?"

"Five months ago. I got tested after. I'm clean, in case you were worried. Haven't touched a woman since then. It's never been anything more than needing a bit of affection for a half hour or so. My hand hasn't always been enough. Sometimes loneliness sets in, and I get desperate enough to put my dick in a random woman, in the hopes it will make me feel better for a short while. Never does, but I kept trying anyway. I usually last anywhere from three to six months before I give in to the temptation." He ran a hand through his hair. "I'm not some young kid who runs around putting his dick in any available hole. The girls at the clubhouse don't really hold any appeal for me until I'm desperate enough for some human contact."

I placed my hands on his chest, feeling the steady thump of his heartbeat. "I've never been with anyone, Forge. If we aren't counting what those boys did to me that night, then consider me a virgin. Just one who has a kid and no longer has a hymen. But I have one more

question... If you haven't been seeing anyone, why did
you have the ring with you?"

He moved in closer, his cock pressed between us.
The feel of how hard, and how big he was, sent my
heart racing. I hadn't exactly seen naked men before, so
I had nothing to compare him to. But he felt a little
bigger than what I'd consider average. I'd been curious
and once read the typical penis measured six inches. I
nearly snickered just thinking of that word and Forge
at the same time. Penis. Too clinical. Made me feel like
I was in sex ed class in high school all over again. No,
that word didn't belong in this situation. Cock was
better.

"Look at me, Whisper." I lifted my gaze to his.
"First, the ring. I carry it with me. No idea why, but
I'm glad I did. Otherwise, I wouldn't have had it today
and it belongs on your finger. Second, are you telling
me I'll be the first man to touch you? The first to give
you pleasure?"

His words thrilled me. He hadn't had a
girlfriend. Hadn't wanted to give the ring to anyone.
And I loved the idea that we were destined to be
together. I'd always envisioned Forge as the man I'd
grow old with. Then my life had turned to shit and I'd
run. Hadn't stopped me from dreaming things could
be different. I felt all warm and fuzzy. Whatever the
reason, he was mine now, and I was his. Nothing else
mattered.

I nodded. "I'd been saving myself. They took so
much from me that night."

Forge kissed me, his tongue flicking against my
lips until I opened and let him in. The taste of him
made my knees weak and my nipples hardened as he
took control. Any fears I'd ever had vanished. He'd
been the only man I'd ever wanted. I clung to him as

he devoured my mouth, giving my lip a quick bite here and there as he kissed me breathless.

"Want to put my mark on you," he said, sinking his teeth into my shoulder just enough to sting. "Want the world to know you're mine."

I tipped my head to the side, baring my neck. He growled before sucking at the tender skin. It hurt just enough I knew it would leave a mark that would last a few days. Forge seemed more than satisfied with his handiwork. He smiled as he rubbed a finger along the sore spot.

"Don't some clubs make their women get tattoos?" I asked.

"Yeah. It's not something the Reckless Kings require, but you'll get a property cut." He kissed me again, softer this time. "You haven't said my name yet, angel. Not since we said our vows. We're alone. You don't have to call me Forge when no one else is around."

"It's hard for me to think of you as Victor after calling you Forge for so long. Not to mention, you don't look like a Victor. I picture someone stuffy when I think of that name. Maybe a librarian or something."

He smiled. "Definitely not a librarian. You can call me whatever you want, Whisper."

"We're not having sex for the first time in the shower, are we?" I asked. Although, my body was definitely on board. I ached for him. Wanted to feel his cock inside me. He'd wanted to mark me? I couldn't think of a better way for him to do it than to fuck me.

"No, baby. I'm going to help you wash, then I'll rinse off the road dust, and we'll head to bed. As much as I want to fuck you until neither of us can walk, I don't think now is the time. As excited as Jacob was, he could wake up during the night or real early in the morning. Don't want him seeing anything he shouldn't. You disappointed to not get a real wedding night?"

I shook my head. "No. Well, maybe a little. I understand why, though. Can I at least touch you?"

He backed up a little and held his arms out to his sides. "Touch me anywhere you want. I'm all yours."

I reached out and wrapped my hand around his hard cock. He hissed in a breath and tipped his head back as I stroked him. The skin was surprisingly soft. I tightened my hold on him and worked my hand faster.

"Whisper." He groaned and opened his eyes. "I'm going to come if you keep that up."

I paused. "Can I do that? Make you come?"

He nodded. "If that's what you want."

I stared at his cock. "Can I use my mouth?"

He muttered something that sounded like *fucking killing me*. Looking up again, I caught the quick jerk of his head and knelt down on the bottom of the tub. The hard surface bit into my knees, but I didn't care. I wet my lips before flicking my tongue over the head of his cock. I felt him twitch in my grasp and knew I needed a better taste.

I eased my lips around the head and sucked lightly. He tasted a little salty as I worked more of him into my mouth. I'd barely gotten halfway down when I felt his fingers grip my hair. He pumped his hips twice and came, the hot fluid filling my mouth so fast I couldn't manage to swallow it all. I felt it run from the corners of my lips down my chin as I tried to choke it all down.

I blinked rapidly, sucking in a huge breath when he pulled out. I swiped the remaining cum off my face and got to my feet. I'd never given a blow job before and had no idea if I'd done it right or not. He'd come, but maybe he'd just been too close already? I wanted to ask, and yet I didn't. What if he never wanted me to do that again? His taste hadn't been unpleasant, and I wanted to suck him off over and over.

Forge backed me to the wall and reached between my legs, his fingers stroking over the lips of my pussy. He spread me open and swiped his fingers over my clit. Oh, God! No one had ever touched me before. Well, they had even though I hadn't been awake for it. *No, you won't think about that night right now!* I gave myself a mental shake and focused on Forge.

"You ever play with yourself, baby?" he asked.

"Y-Yes."

"Show me," he demanded, drawing his hand back. "I want to watch you come."

I parted my thighs more and cupped my pussy. No one ever watched me touch myself. It seemed to be a day for a lot of firsts. My nipples hardened at the look in his eyes. I spread myself open and circled my clit, trying to draw the pleasure out. Sometimes I made myself come fast, just to get a little relief. Others I tried to make it last as long as possible.

Forge leaned in again, bracing his arms on either side of me. His gaze stayed locked between my legs. I struggled to breathe, never having felt so turned on in my life. Who'd have known it would feel so naughty to have him watch me get myself off?

"Know what I want to do to you?" he asked.

"N-No."

"I want to suck those pretty nipples until they're so hard they ache. I want to pinch and tug on them until you're begging me to fuck you."

"Oh, God." I closed my eyes a moment, picturing him doing that very thing.

"I'm going to fuck you nice and slow. Long, deep strokes. I want to watch you stretch to take me. Hold your thighs open and pound that sweet little pussy."

"Forge!"

"I won't stop until you've come all over me at least twice, then I'll flip you over. My cock will go in deeper in that position. Did you know that?"

"No. No, I didn't." I whimpered as my fingers worked my clit faster.

"I'll ride that tight little pussy until I fill it with my cum. Then I'm going to watch as it leaks out of you. Every time I get hard that night, I'm going to fuck you. By morning, you'll be thoroughly used, sore in all the right places, and later that night you'll be asking me for more." He leaned in even closer, his lips near my ear. "Come for me, Whisper. Come right fucking now."

I cried out as he pulled away. I felt his finger stretch me open as he worked my pussy. I'd never put anything inside me, and it burned a little. It didn't take much to make me come a second time, and he added another finger. Stretching me open. I ground against his hand, wanting more. He thrust his fingers a little harder and I nearly saw stars. I wanted...wanted... "Oh, God. Forge, don't stop."

"So fucking beautiful," he murmured. "You have no idea how badly I want to fuck you. I want to own every inch of you, sweet girl. There isn't a part of you I don't want to claim. You going to let me?"

I nodded, nearly mindless with pleasure as another orgasm started to build.

"I mean *every* part, Whisper. I already came in your mouth. I'm going to come in this sweet little pussy. And I'm going to come in your ass. I bet you'll be nice and tight."

His words set me on fire. The naughtiness of it all had me whimpering. I'd read books where they had anal sex. Not once had it ever turned me on. Until Forge said he wanted to put his cock there. Now I couldn't think of anything else. I needed him to claim every part of me, just like he said.

He didn't stop working his fingers until I'd come again. My knees felt weak, and the world spun a bit. Forge had been right that our first time shouldn't be in the shower, but I ached so much for him that I didn't care anymore.

"Please." I held his gaze. "Make me yours... Victor."

He shut off the water and lifted me out of the tub and carried me over to the counter. It felt cold under my ass cheeks, and I gasped, leaning back on my hands. He spread my thighs wide and stared at me like a starving man.

"How do you feel about more kids?" he asked. "Because I don't have any condoms with me."

I'd never given much thought to having another baby. I'd thought I'd always be alone. But kids with Forge? Sign me up! I had no doubt he'd be an amazing father, and the thought of making those babies with him? Yes, please! "I don't want any barriers between us."

He reached up and fisted a handful of my hair, tipping my head back. "That what you want? My cum inside you? Want me to fuck you so good I knock you up?"

"Yes! I need you. I need... need..."

He kissed me hard and deep. "I'll give you that and more."

He lined his cock up with my pussy and slowly sank inside me. I cried out, feeling as if he might split me in two. "Too big!"

He chuckled, the sound dark and raspy. "Oh, you'll take me, sweet girl. This pussy is mine. *You're* mine. And I'm not as big as you think. You're just really fucking tight. Rub your clit again."

I reached down and did as he said. It didn't take long before I'd taken all of him. Forge took his time, claiming me slowly. Every thrust was both torture and pure bliss. The way he watched me, the hunger in his eyes, nearly undid me. I wanted the moment to last forever.

"Come for me, baby. Come on my cock."

It was as if his words released something inside me and I cried out his name, my pussy clenching down on him. He gripped my hips and took me faster, not stopping until I felt the heat of his cum filling me up. His cock twitched inside me as he pressed his forehead to mine.

"You okay, angel?" he asked.

"I'm yours now. Completely yours." I smiled. "I'm perfect."

"That all you ever wanted? To be mine?"

His words made me feel silly. Women didn't think like that anymore, did they? They wanted careers, to make a name for themselves. Or at least the girls I'd gone to high school with had been that way. But me? No, I'd only ever wanted to belong to Forge. To have a family with him.

"Is that stupid?"

He shook his head. "Makes me feel like a fucking king. Having someone sweet as you want to be mine? I won the lotto. Just hope you don't regret your decision one day. I'm a lot older than you."

"You've always treated me right, Forge. The boys my age did something horrible to me. Age is just a number. Yeah, some people might look at us funny, or say our relationship is disgusting. But none of it matters. You're the kindest, bravest man I know, aside from Dad, and I'm lucky that I'm yours. I know you'll never hurt me, that you'll keep me safe, and I've already seen how great you are with Jacob."

"You're right about that disgusting part. Beast and Lyssa have heard it, same with Hawk and Hayley, and even Ranger and Danica. They've had people come up to them and say they were sick for being with someone young enough to be their kid." He sighed. "That going to bother you if it happens to us?"

"No. They don't know our story, what I went through, how you saved me. How can anyone judge me for my actions when they haven't walked in my shoes? Until they've suffered the way I have, they can't say anything. And even then, not everyone deals with crap the same way. Just because I handled things different from them doesn't make my way wrong." He kissed me again, his lips lingering a moment as he pulled out. I felt the rush of our mingled release slipping from my body and wondered if I should take another shower. "You're my hero, Forge. Always have been, always will be."

"Come on, angel. Let's clean up and get some sleep."

"What about the club?" I asked.

"I'll deal with them tomorrow. If they call looking for me before then, I'll talk to them. Otherwise, it's just you and me tonight." He smiled. "Until our son decides he's had enough sleep."

"I like that. Our son." I hugged him tight, not wanting to ever let him go. "Our battle is just starting, isn't it?"

"I'm afraid so. Not just with the club. Tommy is

out there somewhere. He might give us a wide berth and move on with his life, but I somehow doubt that will be the case. He's a whiny little bitch and probably blames you and the club for his prison sentence. Never mind one of his dumbass friends sent out a video of their assault on you. If you'd been a little younger, they'd have gotten time for child pornography too. He's probably not too happy about his time locked up either. The club made sure he and the others suffered every fucking day."

I sighed. "Yeah, I think we need sleep. It's exhausting just thinking about it all, and I have to admit, a bit frightening too. I'm scared of what will happen tomorrow. Terrified the club won't accept me back, even if we *are* legally married. Tommy is only a small part of it."

"I'll keep you safe, Whisper. You and Jacob both. You're my family. My wife and kid. No one's taking either of you from me. Not even Beast."

"You say that now. What if they give you an ultimatum? Leave us, or leave the club?"

He winced and I knew he was thinking about exactly *how* he'd have to leave the club. It wouldn't be peaceful. They'd remove the club colors he'd had inked on his back, among other things. I might not know everything about the club life, but I knew enough. If Forge was forced out, it wouldn't be pretty, and could very well kill him. Unless they went easy on him for some reason.

"I'm not leaving you," he said, his jaw firming. "Whatever they do to me, the only way I'm not coming home to you is if I'm in a shallow grave somewhere."

I shivered. "Let's not even say that, okay? I just got you. I'm not ready to lose you."

He turned the water back on and stuck his hand

under the shower spray. "Water's ice-cold now. Guess we used too much hot water earlier."

"We were otherwise occupied." I smiled. "A little cold water won't kill us. We'll wash fast and get to bed. Besides, it was worth it. I've never felt anything like that before."

He cupped my cheek. "I can't promise you love, Whisper. Not sure I remember what it feels like. What I can say is that I'll be faithful to you, and I care about you a great deal. I'd die for you, or for Jacob."

"It's more than I had this morning." I tipped my head to the side, watching him. He might say he would never love me, but I had my doubts. A man didn't offer up his freedom, vow to give his life for yours, if he only *cared*. No, I had a feeling he loved me at least a little. And if not, my heart was full enough for the both of us. I'd adored Forge from the very first day I'd met him, and nothing would ever change that.

Chapter Four

Forge

I ground my teeth together and clenched the phone so tight I worried I'd break the damn thing. I'd known Beast would be pissed. Knew he'd make threats. But he'd gone too fucking far, and even his woman knew it, since I heard Lyssa going off in the background.

"*That woman*, as you called her, is my fucking wife, Beast. And the daughter of Brick. She made a mistake when she left, thinking she needed a clean break and a fresh start. More than that, she was embarrassed. Several of us saw her that night, clothes ripped, her body exposed. Can you blame her for needing distance?"

"She left the club, Forge. Told us to forget she existed."

"No offense, Pres, but fuck you. I didn't forget her for one damn minute, and don't sit there and tell me anyone else did. They might not have said her name, but it didn't mean Whisper ceased to exist."

I heard Beast tell Lyssa it was club business, then a door slammed shut. I had a feeling he'd be paying for that one later. As the daughter of a club President, Lyssa didn't take shit from Beast. Never had, never would.

"Don't you even fucking think of trying to tell me this is a love match," Beast said. "You married her, so I'd let her come back."

"What the hell do you know about it?"

"Forge, I know damn well you've been balls-deep in pussy more times than I can count since she ran off. A man in love doesn't fuck around with other women. At least, not in this club they don't."

I decided to come clean, or at least partially. "You ever noticed I take off for most of the day at least once a month, sometimes more?"

"Son of a bitch," he muttered. "You knew where she was all this time, didn't you?"

"Yep. Followed Brick one of the times he went to see her. She's never been far from my thoughts. I felt like a sick bastard, but after she turned eighteen, I'd started seeing Whisper in a different light. If she'd stuck around, maybe something would have happened between us sooner."

"As in something has happened now, other than you marrying her?" he asked.

"Too soon to know if she's pregnant, but we haven't been using protection." If I was going to fib a bit, might as well let him think I'd been sleeping with her before this. I needed Beast to realize I was all in when it came to Whisper and Jacob. I glanced around, making sure the kid wasn't nearby. "Listen, Jacob thinks he's my biological son. I don't want anyone telling him any different."

Beast cursed. "You don't play fair, Forge. You know damn well if that kid is calling you Daddy there's no fucking way I can tell you not to bring them home with you. Motherfucker! Anyone asks, you ran all this shit by me before you left. I don't need the club thinking I'm losing control."

I winced. I hadn't thought of it that way. I'd only wanted to keep Whisper and Jacob safe, whatever it took. Even if I'd disrespected Beast by going about this the way I had, I'd have never confronted him in front of everyone. Which was why I'd called him during a time I knew he'd likely be at home.

"You know I didn't mean for anything like that to happen, Pres. I respect you, and I'd follow you straight into hell if need be, but when it comes to Whisper and Jacob --"

"I get it," he said, interrupting. "They're your family. I have to admit, Brick will probably be thrilled to have his daughter back home. Not too sure how he'll feel about you being his son-in-law. Seeing as how you're an entire year younger than him and all."

"Brick knows damn well I'd protect Whisper with my life. He may not know we're married, and I'll handle that in person, but he knows I'll keep my family safe."

"I'd planned to have you make a run tomorrow. Since you'll be getting your wife and kid settled, I'll have Wrangler handle it. Want me to ask Hawk to keep an eye on the metal works for a few days?"

"If he wouldn't mind, that would be great."

"Fine. I'll check with him after I send a Prospect your way. You'll need a truck to haul all their shit home. Expect Logan in the next few hours."

"Thanks, Pres." I ended the call and went to find Whisper.

She'd already started packing, and I could hear Jacob's excited chatter as I neared his room. Leaning against the doorjamb, I smiled as I watched the two of them. I'd made a call first thing and had a collection of moving boxes dropped off by the local hardware store.

"Beast is sending someone with a pickup truck. Should be here in a few hours," I said.

"Everything okay?" she asked.

I nodded. I wouldn't tell her how pissed he'd been. I knew the Pres wouldn't say a damn word to her, other than to welcome her home. Not after our conversation. Last thing I needed was her stressing out over whether or not she'd be allowed inside the compound once we got there.

"Want me to finish helping him pack? I figured you'd want to handle your clothes and stuff. I can start on the kitchen next."

"That would be great. There's not really anything in the kitchen I need to keep except for a few plates and cups Jacob likes. I guess it wouldn't hurt to have extra utensils and pans."

I walked over to Jacob's closet and pulled the stuff off the top shelf, setting it on his bed for easier access. "We can take it all, baby. Whatever you decide not to keep, you can donate after we get home. You may hate the stuff I have and want to use yours."

"The furniture..." She cast a glance around Jacob's room, and I understood. Our boy would need his things. Which meant we'd need more than a pickup to handle all this. I pulled out my phone and called Beast back. All he did was growl when the line connected.

"Pres, Jacob is going to need his furniture. Not sure all this and the boxes will fit into the bed of one truck."

"Fuck. All right. I'll send a second one, but I can't spare Iggy or Kye right now. Logan's got a friend who's made a formal request to prospect for us. I've held him off. If he can help Logan get all your family's shit packed up and back here, then we'll call it a trial run. His name is Bronsen."

"Thanks, Beast. Appreciate it."

He grunted and hung up. I pocketed my phone and went back to helping Jacob. As Whisper passed me, I placed my hand on her hip, tugging her closer. The scent of her was enough to make me semi-hard. After kissing her cheek, I lightly nipped her ear, making her giggle.

"Got two trucks coming," I said. "And you'll get

to meet one of our official Prospects, as well as an unofficial one. Beast is letting this be the guy's trial run."

"New Prospects," she murmured. "What happened to Lyle and Tucker?"

"Lyle and Tucker both patched in the year you left, about four months apart. Lyle goes by Samson and Tucker is Cyclops. The place has changed a little since you were last there."

"Should I call Dad?" she asked.

"I'd rather you didn't. I want to talk to him in person. And I have no doubt he's going to come at me swinging. Whatever you do, you and Jacob stay back."

Jacob let out a sound of distress. "Grandpa is going to hit you?"

I sat on Jacob's bed and lifted him onto my lap. He settled against me, his fingers curling into my cut as he held on tight. The kid already had my heart. I kissed the top of his head and tried to reassure him.

"Your grandpa isn't going to be too happy that I married your mom without talking to him first. If he hits me, it's okay. I'll be fine. Don't try to get between us, all right?"

He nodded and buried his face against my chest. I wondered if he'd ever seen two men fighting before. Not that I had any intention of hitting Brick back. I'd let him get in a few punches, then I'd end it as peacefully as possible. I didn't want to hurt him, not for defending his daughter. Hell, the bastard might surprise me and be fine with the entire thing.

"Let's get your stuff packed up so you can pick out a room when we get home." I patted his back. "You can tell me what color you want the walls, and we'll go paint shopping tomorrow."

"Think Grandpa will let me have a room at his

place too?" Jacob asked.

"I bet he will. He'd probably love to have you spend the night once a week, or maybe every other weekend. He's not too far down the road from my place. You know how to ride a bike?"

"Yeah, but I don't have one yet. Momma said it's 'spensive."

I made sure Whisper wasn't lingering. I had no doubt she'd berate me later for what I was about to do, but so be it. "When we get your paint, we'll stop and look at bikes too. No reason you can't ride over to your grandpa's house to say hi when the weather is nice. Just have to let either me or your mom know where you're going. Deal?"

"Yes!" He launched himself out of my arms and started throwing his toys into a box faster than before. It seemed I'd said the magic words. I didn't plan on buying him whatever he wanted whenever he wanted it, but it wasn't every day I gained a son. I figured spoiling him this one time wouldn't be so bad. I'd missed out on a lot of birthdays and Christmases.

By the time Logan and Bronsen arrived with the two trucks, we had both bedrooms packed and ready. It had taken longer than I'd thought, and I hadn't had a chance to work on the kitchen. The Prospects started taking apart Jacob's bed and loaded the furniture in the truck before starting on the boxes. Jacob supervised while Whisper helped me get the rest of their stuff sorted and packed.

"Think he's driving them crazy?" she asked softly as she craned her neck to see Jacob standing out front.

"Probably. Don't worry about it. He's safe. Even if he talks their ears off, they won't let anything happen to him. Especially Logan. I have a feeling he'll be patched in soon. No fucking way he's jeopardizing that."

"All right. Guess I need to get used to trusting more people again. It's been a while."

I tugged her to me and kissed her. Whisper sighed and melted against me. I didn't like her worrying as much as she was. The fact Tommy was on the loose might be concerning, but I had no doubt that Logan and Bronsen would watch Jacob like a hawk. I doubted that fucking douchebag would even think about going up against either man. He seemed to prefer picking on those who were weaker than him. Even in prison, from what I'd heard, he hadn't been all that tough.

Far as I knew, he hadn't had a way to keep tabs on Whisper while he'd been inside. But Tommy's family had a little money, and I wouldn't put it past him to have connections who could help him track her down. I wasn't going to take any chances with my little family.

"When we head back, I'll take the lead. I want you behind me and I'll have Logan and Bronsen bring up the rear in the two trucks. We're going straight to my house, and while you supervise the unloading and let Jacob pick his room, I'll go talk to your dad. Best to get it out of the way right off."

"No." She bit her lip. "Sorry. It's just... I want you to stay with us. I haven't been to your house in a long time. Jacob hasn't ever seen it, and I think it's important you're there when he decides which bedroom will be his. It's a bonding moment for the two of you."

I smiled a little. "And you're hoping to prolong your dad rearranging my face?"

"Maybe." She snuggled into me. "He has to

know you'd never force me to marry you. If you'd asked me on a date seven years ago, I'd have jumped at the chance. Dad, and probably everyone else, knew it too."

"I liked how you followed me around or showed up at the shop with cookies and other sugary things. It was cute the way you watched me work." I hugged her tight. "You meant a lot to me from the moment I found you, and those feelings only grew over time, Whisper. You know that, right? How much I care about you?"

"I know." She leaned up and kissed me. Just a quick peck, but the fact she instigated it was enough. I hadn't known what to expect last night. Finding out she'd never been with anyone since her attack had made me a little apprehensive. It wouldn't have surprised me if she'd been a crying mess and needed more time. Instead, she'd shocked the hell out of me by taking matters into her own hands, so to speak.

We finished packing the house, buckled an overly excited Jacob into the back of Whisper's car, and hit the road. I'd never traveled with a kid before and hadn't realized we'd have to make a few stops. What shouldn't have taken more than two hours ended up taking three. By the time we pulled through the gates, it was nearing dinnertime. I had no doubt Jacob would be asking about food soon.

The Prospects started to unload the truck while Jacob ran inside and looked around. I showed him the spare bedrooms, neither of which were currently empty.

"Is there one you like?" I asked, placing my hand on his shoulder.

He stood in the hall, looking between the rooms. The indecision on his face gave me an idea. If he didn't like these, maybe he'd like the bonus room. I'd intended to use it as storage for my overstock but hadn't needed the space in a while. It likely had cobwebs hanging from the ceiling.

"Follow me. There's something you might want to see."

He took my hand and I led him back to the living room. I opened the door hidden in the back corner and showed him the space that ran the length of the house. The room would be wide enough to hold a full-size bed and his furniture, when the time came for him to upgrade from a twin. It even had a long, narrow closet.

"I used this for storage so I'm afraid it's a bit dusty. The windows overlook the front yard and the backyard. It's bigger than the other rooms I showed you. And while it might be a bit scary being so far away from where your mom and I will be sleeping, when you're older I think you'll like having this space to yourself."

"It can be my bedroom?" Jacob asked.

"It sure can. We can paint it whatever color you want. Put up posters. Curtains. It's all up to you."

Jacob looked around the room again. He wandered to the rear window and peered out at the backyard before doing the same at the front window. He walked the space, opened the closet, and put his hands on his hips. "Are you and momma giving me a brother or sister?"

My eyebrows went up. "We haven't discussed it much, but it's possible at some point in the future. Does that bother you?"

"No. I always wanted a baby brother. But my friend Timmy had a little sister, and she was really loud all the time."

"If you have this room, you wouldn't be woken up by a crying baby."

He nodded. The kid cracked me up. So grown up for a six-year-old. Then again, he'd probably had to grow up a little fast being in a house with a single mom. Whisper couldn't be everywhere at once, which meant Jacob had to get off the bus and let himself in the house or stay with a neighbor.

"I'll take it," Jacob said.

I couldn't hold back a chuckle. "All right. We'll go to the hardware store tomorrow and you can pick out some paint. Anything else you want for in here?"

His eyes went wide, and he came a little closer. "Could I have a TV in my room? There's lots of space for one."

Something told me Whisper had already told him no in the past. I didn't know if it was because of the cost of a TV, or another reason. As much as I wanted to give him what he wanted, I didn't dare say anything without consulting his mom first. I'd only been his dad for one night.

"I'll talk to your mom about it."

He huffed. "She'll say no."

I ruffled his hair. "If she says no, then I'm sorry, buddy. It means no TV in here. Maybe when you're a little older."

"Forge!" I winced, knowing exactly who was outside bellowing my name. It seemed it was time to confront Brick.

"Grandpa sounds mad," Jacob said, seeming to shrink in on himself.

I knelt in front of him. "Hey, it's okay. Your grandpa sometimes yells, but he'd never hurt you or your mom. You know that right?"

Jacob nodded.

"I did something he's not happy about. Whatever happens, know that we both love you, all right?"

Tears filled Jacob's eyes. "Is he going to hit you?"

"Maybe. Remember what we talked about earlier. If he does, I can handle it. Don't get in the way. I wouldn't want you to get hurt by accident."

I lifted Jacob and hugged him. Carrying him through the house, I found Whisper outside, arguing with her dad. I handed Jacob to her and jerked my chin toward the house, telling her to get inside. Her worried gaze held mine and I gave her a reassuring smile.

Once the door shut, Brick came at me, fists swinging. I let him get in a few hits before I caught his hand and gripped it tight enough to get his attention. His chest heaved as he panted for breath. His face had turned red and fury blazed in his eyes.

"You about done?" I asked. "Because Jacob was worried you were going to hurt me."

My words seemed to drain the anger from him. He deflated, casting a glance toward the house. "Why are they here?"

"You didn't tell Whisper about Tommy being out. I went to check on her. Didn't plan on her seeing me. When she did, I had a choice to make. Stay and face her or run like a little bitch."

Brick sighed. "The two of you were always close. Shouldn't surprise me if anyone was going to seek her out it would be you. How long have you known where she was?"

"A while. Been keeping an eye on her, staying out of sight."

"You brought them here to keep them safe, didn't you?" Brick asked.

"Something like that." I folded my arms over my chest. "You know I'll protect them with my life, Brick. I didn't marry Whisper on a whim. I care about her."

"I noticed the ring on her finger," he said.

"Jacob thinks I'm his dad. Whisper and I spun a story for him as to why I haven't met him before now. I don't want anyone telling him different."

Brick seemed to age before my very eyes. "You did that for them?"

"You sound surprised."

"I've worried. Jacob has asked about his dad so many times. Whisper always redirects him without having to come up with an answer. You've given that boy something no one else ever could."

"We good?" I asked.

Brick nodded. "Let me talk to my daughter and grandson."

"Sure thing." I smirked. "Dad."

He flipped me off before heading into my house. I just hoped the rest of the club reacted favorably when it came to Whisper being here. The first fucker who hurt her feelings or made her want to leave was going to get my fist down his throat. Even if it was Beast or Hawk.

Chapter Five

Whisper

Since Jacob wanted paint and other things for his new bedroom, he'd gone to spend the night with my dad. The furniture remained in the bed of one of the trucks with a tarp thrown over it in case it rained. All the boxes had been unloaded and I'd put away my clothes and shoes, after Forge made room for them. Everything else could wait until tomorrow, or even the day after.

I leaned against him on the couch as a movie played. My dad had ordered pizza and stayed to eat with us before taking Jacob back to his place. Now I felt full and incredibly tired. I'd wanted to celebrate with Forge. After Jacob had gone to bed tonight, I'd planned to lure my sexy husband to the bedroom and beg him to have his wicked way with me. Except, now we had the house to ourselves, and I didn't think I could move long enough to walk down the hall.

"Tired, angel?" he asked, his voice a low murmur.

I nodded. "It's been quite the day."

"Come on. We'll get some sleep and make a plan when we get up in the morning." He stood and lifted me into his arms. I held on as he stopped at the front door, twisting the deadbolt into place. He carried me to our bedroom and eased me down. "Need anything?"

"No. I put my bathroom stuff up already, or at least the important things like my toothbrush, comb, and deodorant. Everything else I'll unpack tomorrow." He kissed the top of my head and went over to the dresser. I smiled when I saw him pull out a pair of sweatpants. From a conversation I'd once overheard, I knew he slept naked. "Scared I'll take advantage of you in your sleep?"

"No. Before Brick left, I gave him a spare key to the house. If Jacob wants to come home early in the morning, he'll bring him by. Don't need our son running in here and finding me in bed with his mom while not wearing clothes." He eyed me from head to toe. "Anytime you want to take advantage of me, you're more than welcome to."

My heart melted a little. He'd done so much for us since he'd shown up yesterday. It made me wonder what our lives might have been like if I hadn't run seven years ago. If I'd stayed, would Forge and I have ended up together sooner? How different would Jacob's life have been? I'd told Forge I didn't want to play the what-if game, and yet I couldn't seem to help myself.

It seemed to run on a steady loop in my head. All the things that might have been different. The ways Jacob's life could have been better. He'd have grown up with a club full of men who'd have done anything for him. Instead, I'd been too ashamed to look them in the eye and I'd done the cowardly thing. It hadn't even benefited me in the end. I'd struggled, despite my dad helping when he could. Which meant Jacob had felt the impact, whether it was getting clothes at the thrift store, to eating grilled cheese or hot dogs because we didn't have anything else.

I got ready for bed, pulled on my favorite pajamas, and slid under the covers. Forge lifted his arm and I settled against his side. Placing my hand on his chest, I could feel the thump of his heartbeat. I found it soothing and closed my eyes, hoping I'd fall asleep quickly. It felt like I'd last slept a decade ago. Finding out Tommy wasn't in prison anymore, getting married, then quickly packing and moving had taken its toll on me.

"I'm scared, Forge."

"We'll find him, Whisper, and make sure he can't hurt you or anyone else ever again."

I snuggled closer. He'd known exactly what I'd meant without me having to explain. It had always been like that between us. Even when I'd been a pesky teenager, I'd say something completely random, and he'd answer as if he'd seen inside my head. I hadn't realized how much I'd missed him until I'd looked up yesterday and found him watching me. Leaving the club behind hadn't been all that difficult. My dad had still come to visit. What had hurt was walking away from Forge.

"I'm sorry I ran," I said.

"You did what you thought was best, baby. No one can fault you for that. We'll make the club understand. Don't let any of them make you feel bad, you hear me?"

I nodded. I wouldn't blame them for being angry. They'd done so much for me, given me a home when I didn't have one anymore. When I'd left, I'd cut all ties with them. I hadn't even stopped to think how it had made them feel. I'd been too focused on what I needed to do to survive and move forward with my life.

Except I hadn't really needed to walk away to survive.

Dad had stayed in touch and visited when he could. I'd missed him when he wasn't around, and being on my own had been terrifying, especially since I'd been pregnant and later a single mom. I'd managed to get through school and finish my degree. I'd decided to study business, and my dad had tried to talk me out of it. Not because he thought the degree would be useless, but because of how many people were getting the same degree. For every job I applied to, so did dozens of other people.

"What if it wasn't necessary?" I asked.

"You leaving? You were set to go to school anyway."

"But I could have come home on breaks, or even stayed home and taken classes online." I sighed. "Knowing you'd seen me like that... The others I could have dealt with, eventually. You've always been different, Forge."

"I wanted to kill them. Track them down, make them suffer, and eventually kill them with my bare hands. Then your phone dinged with that damn video. I couldn't make them disappear afterward. Too many people would have asked where they went. You'd have been identified and made a person of interest, which would have put the club in the spotlight."

"You might not have killed them personally, but you did arrange for two of them to never make it out of prison."

He nodded. "Yes, I did. There were plans for Tommy too. The little fucker just got out before I had everything in place."

"Won't it be noticed if he disappears? You said he was out on parole. Someone will be keeping tabs on him, right?"

"He's supposed to check in with a parole officer. Whether he does it or not is another matter. If he doesn't, he can technically go back to prison, assuming they find him. That also means his parole officer has to report it. If they're backlogged, that may not happen anytime soon."

"Jacob will need to be registered for school here. We left so quickly, I didn't get a chance to officially unenroll him and get his records. Will it be safe for him to leave the compound?"

Forge rolled onto his side to face me. "No one is going to hurt Jacob. You have my word."

I trailed my fingers along his jaw. For so long I'd wanted this. It seemed like all my dreams were within reach, as long as Tommy didn't screw everything up. "You can't promise things like that, Forge. You have no control over the universe, only your own actions. We can't be with Jacob every second of the day."

"There's something I want you to consider. Don't disregard it right away."

I had a feeling I wouldn't like what he was about to say. "What?"

"I want you and Jacob to both have GPS trackers. Before you ask, this isn't a SciFi movie. It's not going in your body. I'd put one in the soles of your shoes, in the lining of your purse, the lining of Jacob's backpack, and I want one on your car. They'd be real time trackers, which means it would show me your location no matter the time of day, and I could track the two of you through my phone."

"You do remember I was kidnapped as a child, right?"

He smiled faintly. "I know. I also know you like your freedom. You probably didn't miss the club watching your every move. Then again, if we'd been doing a better job of that, you'd have never been hurt."

"Is that what you need for peace of mind?" I asked.

"It would help. The thought of losing you isn't something I can deal with right now. It hurt enough when you left, and I knew you were alive and well. If someone were to snatch you or Jacob off the street, I think I'd lose my fucking mind trying to get you back."

"Then yes, you can put trackers on our things. Besides, I like the idea of being able to find Jacob quickly if anything were to happen." Maybe some would consider it wrong, but after all I'd been through, if I could prevent my child from suffering a similar fate, then I'd do anything I could. If that meant chipping him like a pet, so be it.

Forge tucked my hair behind my ear. "Thought you were tired."

"I was. My brain won't shut off."

"We should get a TV for in here. Then when you can't sleep, you'd at least be in bed while you watched something."

"Want to take a bath with me? I noticed the tub looked big enough for both of us."

He pressed a kiss to my forehead. "I'll go get the tub ready."

"I have some eucalyptus-scented bath salts in one of my boxes. I'll look for it while you start the bath."

Forge went into the bathroom while I rummaged through my things. I hadn't had a chance to label all the boxes so I had to open three before I found what I wanted. I carried the small jar over to the tub and put a scoop into the water. Forge pulled two towels out from under one of the sinks and set them on the counter. He got into the tub and held out his hand to me. I took it and stepped over into the steamy paradise.

I sank into the water and leaned back against his chest. It didn't take long before I felt his cock start to harden. He didn't do anything more than lightly run his hands up and down my legs or massage my hands. I felt myself relax more and more, and yet it didn't make me the least bit sleepy. If anything, a warmth started to build inside me, and an ache started between my thighs.

"How is it you can touch me so innocently and it makes me want more?" I asked.

"Your body is starved for attention." He nipped my ear. "Could also be you're hyperaware of the fact you're finally mine."

"You sound so cocky."

"Mmm. More like confident. You want me every bit as much as I want you, Whisper. Nothing wrong with that. You have any idea how turned on I get knowing I'm the only one who's given you pleasure?"

"Not quite." He tensed and I knew I needed to soothe his ruffled feathers. "I got myself off sometimes. Just not as well as you do it."

"That right?" he murmured. His hand slipped over my hip and down between my legs. I felt his fingers rub against my pussy before he parted the lips and stroked my clit. "Might need you to prove it."

"Victor... you're not playing fair."

"Fuck! I love hearing my name on your lips." He plunged a finger inside me before rubbing my clit again. "All's fair in love and war. Come for me, pretty girl. Show me how much you love my touch."

"You know I do! I've never wanted anyone else to touch me." I thrust against his hand, needing more. I wanted him inside me. "Please."

"Please what?"

"Stop teasing me! You know what I need, what I want."

"Get up."

I stood on trembling legs and got out of the tub. Forge followed, yanking the towels off the counter and briskly drying us both before nudging me back into the bedroom. I crawled onto the bed and sat on my knees facing him.

"On your back, Whisper. Legs spread. You want me? You better be ready to take everything I've got to give. I'm not great at going slow or being gentle."

I sprawled in the center of the bed and placed my hands over my head. Only with Forge would I ever let myself be this vulnerable. I wanted him to know I offered all of myself to him. Forge settled over me, the weight of his body pressing me into the mattress. I stared up into his eyes and felt my heart racing. Whatever he asked of me, I knew I'd give it to him. He didn't scare me. With Forge, I knew I was safe. He'd take care of me, no matter the situation.

"You don't need to be anything other than yourself," I said.

He reached between us, sinking a finger inside me again. "So fucking wet. You ready to scream my name?"

I nodded. "More than."

I felt his cock press inside me, stretching me wide. I moaned as he slid in deeper. He braced his weight on one arm, though his body still held me immobile under his. His other hand wrapped around my wrists. The way his gaze scanned my face, I could tell he was waiting to see if I'd freak out. If anyone else had pinned me like this, I might have. I trusted Forge with my life. My body. My everything.

He rocked into me, slowly at first. His thrusts were shallow, as if he were testing me to make sure I hadn't lied. It didn't take long before he was pounding into me, his cock sliding in deep. The friction of his body against my clit and my nipples had me so close. On the next stroke, I came, calling out his name.

"Victor! Don't stop! Please don't stop!"

The headboard slammed against the wall as he took what he wanted. He growled, his body tightening, and then he was coming. He slid his hand down to my hip and squeezed. "I didn't hurt you?"

"No. It was perfect."

He kissed me, his lips feeling like a brand against mine. Even now, I craved more. I didn't think I'd ever tire of him touching me. I squeezed his cock, and he drew back, giving me a smirk.

"Sorry, baby. You married an old man. It's going to be a bit before I can go again."

"You're not old," I said. "Yes, there's nineteen years between us. But you know what? No one has ever treated me as good as you do. There isn't a thing I'd change about you, Forge. Not even your age."

"You may change your mind in twenty years. You'll be forty-five and I'll be in my sixties."

"Are you going to stop finding me beautiful?"

"What? Of course not!"

"Will you not want to touch me anymore?"

"Don't be an idiot," he muttered. "Touching you is quickly becoming my favorite thing to do. I'll want you until the day I die."

"Then I don't see a problem."

He pulled out and rolled to his side, apparently not caring about the mess slipping from between my legs and onto the sheets. "You'll hit your sexual prime and be able to go for hours. I'll be lucky to get it up once a day and last more than ten minutes."

I snorted. "Bullshit. Besides, if you're that worried about it, there are other ways we could have fun in the bedroom. We could buy sex toys. I've never used any, but it might be hot if you were the one controlling them."

"You'd be open to trying out a few toys?"

"With you? Yes. But I want it to be something we do together. Playing with them on my own doesn't sound nearly as fun."

"Then I guess I'd better place an order tomorrow. We'll find out what you like and go from there."

I curled into his side and breathed in his scent. "Thank you. I don't mean for that, or even the sex. You didn't have to come find me yesterday. And when I saw you, you could have left without talking to me. I've missed you so much."

"Missed you too, angel. Get some sleep. We'll have another busy day tomorrow."

I closed my eyes and cuddled with the sexiest man I'd ever met and wondered how I'd gotten lucky enough to call him mine.

Chapter Six

Forge

The fact a week had passed and no one had seen Tommy, or heard from him, put me on edge. He hadn't met with his parole officer, hadn't accessed his accounts. It was like the fucker had vanished. Except grown-ass men didn't disappear unless they had some help. So the question remained, had someone assisted him with leaving the area? Were they hiding him? Or had he pissed off the wrong person and was already rotting in a grave somewhere? As much as I wanted to bury the fucker myself, knowing he wouldn't hurt Whisper again would be good enough.

"Nothing?" I asked.

Shield shook his head. "Sorry, brother. I've searched. I can't even find him using the cameras around town. No traffic cams, store security footage… nothing. If he's out there walking around, it has to be with a new face. Wire and Lavender even hacked into the systems and used their facial recognition program to search for him. They came up empty too."

Well, fuck. If those two couldn't find the asshole, it didn't bode well. He could be anywhere. I'd thought for sure he'd come for Whisper. He hadn't had an easy time in prison. If I were in his position, I'd want revenge. I didn't think for one second that prick had grown a conscience in the pen. No, he was up to something. I just didn't know what it was. Yet.

"Keep looking. He has to be somewhere. I want Whisper to sleep well at night and not worry what might happen when she leaves the compound. With Jacob in school, it's not like the two of them can stay locked up here indefinitely."

"You know we won't give up, Forge. Whisper

and Jacob are family."

"Thanks. Not sure everyone sees it that way." I ran a hand over the beard slowly growing in. I needed to shave, but who the fuck had time? Between my new family, trying to find Tommy, the shit I handled for the club, and working at the shop, I was already spread a little thin.

"They'll come around. Lyssa, Hayley, and Danica all love her. Which means you've got their men in your corner. Not to mention Brick is her dad, so naturally he'll be on your side. The newer members seem to like Whisper well enough."

"I know, and I'm grateful. Really. I'm just not sure I can handle the remarks the others think I don't hear. They're starting to run their mouths around the damn club whores too. I won't have those bitches badmouthing my woman."

Shield sighed. "You know damn well why they're being so catty. You haven't been to the clubhouse since you got back. Even if you didn't take any of them up on their offers the last several months or more, you were at least there. They thought they had a shot at getting into your bed, and maybe staying there forever. Then you show up married and avoid the parties... They'll get over it, or Whisper will need to confront them. You know it's the only way."

"I know. I need to take her over there, even if it's just for a half hour. She needs to show them she's not a pushover."

"Think she'd stand up to them?" he asked. "She seems so quiet and reserved."

"Someone tries to put their hands on me, I think she'll fight back." I smiled. "I've made sure she knows I don't want anyone but her. No reason she'd let them get away with anything."

"Where's Whisper right now?" he asked.

"She and Danica went to pick up Jacob from school. It's why I'm hanging out near the gate. Want to make sure they get home safe."

Shield shoved his hands into his pockets and rocked back on his heels. "There's something I need to tell you."

Those words never bode well. I sighed and motioned for him to keep talking. Whatever he'd done or heard, might as well get it handled now. There were times this past week I'd wished I wasn't the Sergeant at Arms for the club.

"I know you married Whisper legally," he said. "And you've claimed Jacob as your son. So I decided to make sure no one ever questioned it."

"Explain."

"I hacked into the birth records. If anyone goes looking, it will show you're Jacob's father, and I changed his last name to match yours. Which meant I had to hack into both schools too so the documents would match. Would have done it sooner, but I waited to see how Beast and Hawk would handle your marriage. Didn't want to do anything that might piss off the Pres and VP."

"They keep paper copies of everything. You can't fix those through your computer," I pointed out.

He waved a hand. "Got it handled."

"Do I want to know?"

"Probably not. The less you know the better. Plausible deniability and all that."

"Jesus," I muttered. "You start hanging out with lawyers all of a sudden?"

His ears turned red, and he cleared his throat, refusing to hold my gaze. Holy shit. He really had been hanging out with a lawyer. Had to be a woman. Snake might be into both men and women, but as far as I knew, Shield only liked pussy.

"Your love life better not fuck over the club." I shook my head. "Beast know you're dating a lawyer?"

"I wouldn't exactly say we're dating."

"Right. So, the Pres know you're *fucking* a lawyer?"

"No." Shield sulked. "You know he'll tell me to back off."

"Brother, unless you're planning to claim that woman, I'd not screw with Beast on this one. There's a reason he doesn't like lawyers hanging around, or us spilling club secrets during sex. You want pussy? There's plenty inside," I said pointing to the clubhouse.

"I know. I know! It's just... There's something about her. She's smart. Like really smart. And she's a wild cat in the bedroom. I have the scars to prove it. The women who come around here act like they don't have two brain cells in their heads. I like being able to have a real conversation with a woman."

"You can date someone with a brain in their heads without it being someone who walks on the right side of the law. Or at least someone who isn't bound to uphold it. No lawyers, no cops, no judges." I saw Danica's truck coming toward the gate and I walked over. "Do what you want, Shield. But when Beast tears you a new one, don't say I didn't warn you."

He waved me off and went inside the clubhouse. The gates opened and Danica pulled through, stopping when she saw me. I could hear Jacob shouting and smiled as I opened the rear door. After I unbuckled him from his booster seat, I lifted him into my arms.

"How was school?" I asked.

"It was great! At recess, we played kickball. Then

I got to go to art today and I drew a picture of our family. You, me, Momma, and Grandpa. I didn't get to bring it home today, but my teacher said I can later."

"I can't wait to see it. What do you want to do this afternoon?"

Whisper made her way to my side, going up on her tiptoes to kiss my cheek. "Dad is coming to get him. Said he has a surprise for Jacob."

I knew exactly what the surprise was. A rather elaborate playset with a clubhouse, slide, two swings, a seesaw, and a rope ladder. Except the one Brick had purchased had blackened wood with orange plastic for the swings and such. He'd put metal Harley Davidson signs up on some of the posts and had even brought in some of that expensive play turf that would keep Jacob from getting hurt too bad if he fell. Brick hadn't spared any expense.

It also meant I needed to do something at my house now. I'd put in a fence out back, but not done much else. I'd ordered some supplies this morning for delivery later in the week. By next Monday, if not sooner, Jacob would have a custom-built sandbox at home, as well as a cover for it. Since he'd enjoyed kickball at school, I wondered if he'd like a soccer goal out back. Nothing permanent, but I'd seen some kid-sized ones you could fold up and put away when they weren't being used.

"So it's just you and me for the afternoon?" I asked.

She nodded and leaned into my side. "Whatever shall we do?"

Since she'd mentioned it... I glanced at the clubhouse. The sooner she confronted the club whores, the better. She knew about them, since she'd lived here before. I didn't think she'd ever spoken to them much.

Brick would have had a damn fit if she had. I knew I hadn't taken her anywhere near them before. Then again, she'd been a teenager.

Brick pulled up in his truck and I carried Jacob over. After I buckled him into his booster seat, I took Whisper's hand and started walking to the clubhouse. "We're going to grab a drink."

"In there?" she asked. "Are you sure that's a good idea?"

I stopped and turned to face her. "Baby, you know how this all works. We might have sheltered you a bit, and I know you weren't allowed at the clubhouse unless it was a family event, but you're aware of the club whores and their purpose."

"So you want to go introduce me to them?" Her brow furrowed.

"No. We're going to go sit at the bar. It won't take long before one of them decides to start something."

"Ah. And you want me to what? Fight for you? Throw a punch? Pull their hair?"

I smiled. "Something like that. You need to let them know you aren't a pushover. Show them you can hold your own, and that you won't stand for them coming onto me."

"Fine. Let's get this over with."

She grumbled under her breath as she marched up the steps and through the door. I covered my mouth so I wouldn't laugh. She looked so resigned. If I hadn't thought this was necessary, I'd have never pushed her. I went inside and found her already seated at the bar. I took the spot next to her and eyed the drink already sitting in front of her.

"What the hell is that?" I asked.

"Virgin daquiri." She lifted her eyebrows.

"Unless you'd rather me drink alcohol while not knowing for sure if you've already knocked me up."

A warmth spread through me at the thought of her carrying my kid. Yeah, I'd claimed Jacob, but I'd missed out on everything. Seeing her belly swell, going to visits with her, being there for the birth. I'd missed Jacob's first words, the first time he crawled or walked, and so much more. If we had a baby together, I'd get to be there for all of it.

"I know that look," she said. "You're about to do your best to get me pregnant, aren't you?"

I just grinned and didn't say a word. Since she'd planted the idea, damn right I planned to knock her up. She didn't have to work unless she wanted to, so she needn't worry about taking maternity leave. She could easily stay home with Jacob and any other kids we had. If she really wanted to use her degree, she could help me find ways to make the metal works more profitable. I made a killing off the custom pieces I created, but it took so long to complete one project, I needed to get customers in to buy the ready-made items already stocked.

I felt a light touch on my shoulder and saw Paris out of the corner of my eye. I'd never touched her. Hadn't stopped her from trying to get into my pants. The woman was tall, nearly six feet, and I'd always preferred smaller women. Out of all the women to start something, I'd hoped it wouldn't be her. Would Whisper go toe to toe with someone bigger than her? Did I even want her to?

"Forge, aren't you going to get me a drink?" Paris asked.

"Nope."

She ran her fingers over my jaw, and I tried not to snarl at her. "I can pay you for it any way you want."

"Do you deal with this every time you come here?" Whisper asked.

I nodded. At least Paris had most of her clothes on. Could be worse. It was early enough in the day the girls weren't parading around completely naked. Yet. Although, the bra Paris wore didn't hide much. Neither did her shorts. How the hell had she gotten here in those things? It was cold as fuck outside thanks to a recent weather shift.

"I've missed seeing you around here," Paris said, leaning into me. "You haven't even been in for a drink lately."

"Been busy."

Paris ran her nails up my thigh. Whisper groaned and pressed her forehead to the bar. "This is ridiculous."

"Come on, Forge. I can make you feel *so* good," Paris said.

Whisper slid her drink over and used her stool to get up onto the bar. She turned to face the room and let loose a shrill whistle that had me wincing. Although, I couldn't complain too much. I'd taught her how to do that.

"Excuse me!" Whisper shouted. "May I have your attention for a moment?"

Someone shut off the music and the murmur of voices died down.

"I'm sure you all know Forge," Whisper said, her voice still louder than usual. "There's a reason he hasn't been around lately. He's been with me."

Paris sneered up at Whisper. "What the hell would he want to do that for?"

Whisper smiled at me. "Because I'm his wife."

I heard a shriek from somewhere behind me.

Didn't care who'd made the sound. The woman on the bar had my full attention. Paris dug her nails into me harder, and I reached over, gripping her hand tight enough to hurt without causing lasting damage. When I released her, she backed off.

"So that's what I wanted to say. He's mine. Keep your paws to yourself."

I reached up and held her hand as she got off the bar and sat on the stool again. "Not quite what I had in mind, but whatever works, angel."

"I'm not big on fights. Besides, can't you just avoid this place?" she asked.

"Not entirely. There will be times I come have a drink with my brothers. Doesn't mean I'm going to touch any of the women here."

Copper wandered over and leaned against the bar on the other side of Whisper. "Have to say that was rather anticlimactic. I figured there'd be some hair pulling, screaming. Something."

Carina approached, moving slow and seeming unsure. She stopped a few feet away. "Is it okay if I speak to your wife, Forge?"

"Up to her," I said.

Whisper turned to face the woman. She didn't get up, didn't offer to shake her hand. Just stared her down. Carina twitched and shifted on her feet. I'd never seen a club whore so uncomfortable before.

"My name is Carina," the woman said. "I just wanted to say I respect what you just did. You didn't come in calling us names or trying to hit us."

Whisper glanced at me before focusing on Carina again. "You're people same as everyone else. Why would I do all that unless you provoked me?"

"Paris was touching your man. For some, that's enough reason."

Whisper stood and moved closer to Carina. The woman looked ready to run at any moment. I watched them in the mirror over the bar. If Whisper needed me to step in, I would. Until then, I'd let her handle it how she saw fit. I wouldn't always be there to rescue her. Hell, I hadn't been there when it counted. *Don't go there.*

"If she hadn't backed down, then I'd have tried something different," Whisper said. "I'm not going to condemn you for the choices you've made. Your reasons for wanting to be here, for sleeping with multiple men, are just that… *your* reasons. It's not my business. As long as no one tries to touch Forge, then I don't have a problem with any of you."

Carina looked like she might cry for a moment before straightening her spine. "Thank you. None of us will go near him. What you did… it means a lot."

Whisper gave her a slight smile and sat beside me again, sipping her drink. I put my arm around her waist and tugged her closer to me. "Proud of you."

"For being a decent human being?" she asked.

"No. You do that every day. I'm proud of the fact you considered why those women are here. Not sure anyone, even myself and my brothers, have really given it any thought. They're here and willing. Always been enough."

"You know, some women may just really like sex and want to spread the love around. For others…" She cuddled against me. "Maybe things aren't so great when they leave this place. They have heat in the winter and air conditioning in the summer. I'm sure you offer them food and drinks. At least they know you aren't going to hurt them or kill them. Out there, if they were to use sex for those things or some cash, they'd be taking their lives into their hands."

Well, fuck me sideways. It seemed Whisper had grown up in more ways than one. I didn't realize she'd become so insightful. She'd taken one look at these women and seen something none of us had. Now that she'd brought it up, I had to wonder... why *were* they here?

The door slammed open, and Shield stumbled inside. His eyes were wide and frantic, his hair standing on end. He nearly ran toward me, and my gut clenched. If he was this worked up, then it wasn't good news.

"We have a problem," Shield said.

"Clearly. Church?"

He nodded. "I already messaged the other officers."

Carina stepped forward again, wringing her hands. "Um, I know women usually aren't allowed in Church. I can sit with your wife, if you want?"

"Thanks, Carina." I kissed Whisper's cheek. She squeezed my hand before I walked off. Maybe she'd figure out why some of the women decided to party with us. If they were here to get off the streets, I'd look into a way to help them. It was the least I could do.

Chapter Seven

Whisper

The more I spoke with Carina, the more I liked her. I hadn't realized she was older than me. Most of the women here were nineteen to twenty-three. Except Carina. And her reason for being here broke my heart. I knew I couldn't let her keep doing this. She might not be selling herself for money, but it was close enough, and I could tell it was weighing on her.

"Why didn't you tell anyone you needed help?" I asked. "That's kind of what these guys do."

"You don't understand. There's more to my situation." Carina started to shred one of the bar napkins. "If they found out, I'd be in so much trouble."

"Then tell me what's going on. If the club can't help you, we'll find another way. Is there anything I can do?"

"You're so nice," Carina whispered. "No one's been nice to me in a long time."

"Why are you scared?" I asked.

Her gaze strayed to the men sitting at a table in the corner. Since they weren't officers, they hadn't gone into Church with Shield and Forge. Whatever she didn't want to talk about, did it have to do with one of them? Wrangler, Satyr, Cyclops, and Copper talked as they drank their beer. I didn't think any of them would hurt Carina, or any other woman.

"Did one of them do something to you?" I asked, lowering my voice.

"What? No! Why would you even say such a thing?"

"Because you're acting like they're going to murder you if you say whatever is on your mind."

"I come here every day because whoever is

working the grill lets me take home some food." Her hands shook as she pressed them to the bar. "If I tell you my secret, you can't tell him."

"Forge?"

She shook her head. "No. Not your husband. You can't tell Snake."

"He never speaks to me so that's not an issue."

"I don't want you to think badly of me when I tell you this, but... I'm not sure I can keep it to myself anymore either. One of the nights I came here four years ago, there was a party raging. Like, one of the biggest I'd ever seen. I hooked up with Snake that night, and someone else." She rolled her lips into her mouth and pressed down a moment. "Snake likes men and women equally. That night, I gave myself to him and his... whatever they were."

"And you think the club will care?" I asked, not sure where this was going.

"I got pregnant. It had to be that night. I woke the next morning with my thighs all sticky. I don't know if they didn't use condoms every time, or if one broke."

"Why didn't you tell Snake? I'm sure he'd have helped support the two of you."

Tears swam in Carina's eyes. "There were three babies. One was stillborn. My little boy."

Carina started sobbing and I didn't know what to do. I awkwardly hugged her. I couldn't imagine losing my baby. What would I have done if Jacob hadn't been breathing when I'd had him? What if he'd already been gone? I still didn't know why she hadn't told Snake about the other two children. He wasn't a complete asshole.

"What about the other two?" I asked.

"Girls. Their names are Clover and Poppy.

They're three now." She pulled out her phone and showed me a picture. I knew without a doubt their father wasn't Snake. Whoever the other man had been, he had to be the sperm donor. Neither girl looked anything like him.

"Would you like me to talk to Snake with you?" She started to protest, and I held up a hand. "Wait and hear me out. We can say that you've thought about the other man a lot over the years and wanted to know how to get in touch with him. Wouldn't hurt to try, right? Worst thing that can happen is Snake says no."

"He's not even here," she argued.

I motioned the Prospect over. "Logan, could you ask Snake to come to the clubhouse?"

He gave a sharp nod. "I'll call him now. Anything in particular I should tell him?"

"Whatever will get him here."

He gave me a thumbs-up and walked off. He must have succeeded in reaching Snake since the man walked through the door about fifteen minutes later. He looked windblown and I had to wonder if he'd been out riding. I waved him over to the bar, ignoring the scowl on his face.

"What the hell do you want?" he demanded.

Ouch. All right. Must be one of the men who didn't want me here. I knew a few hadn't come around yet. Just hadn't realized Snake was one of them. This was going to make things a little more difficult.

"Hi, Snake. Um. Carina needed to ask you something." I nudged her, hoping she'd speak up.

"I got called in because a club whore wanted to ask a question?" He folded his arms over his chest. "By a traitor who walked out on the club?"

I winced and hated he felt that way. "This isn't about me, Snake. It's about Carina."

"Fine." He held Carina's gaze. "What do you need to ask me?"

"Four years ago, I came to a party and, um…" Her cheeks flushed. "I went off with you and another man. Stayed with the two of you all night."

Snake's eyebrows shot up into his hairline. "I remember."

Carina gave me a helpless look and I sighed, knowing she wasn't going to ask. "She needs to know who the other man was."

Snake smiled. "Why? You want to go another round? I can call him up. See if he's available."

"That's not… I mean…" Carina shrank in on herself. Naturally, Snake would think she wanted to party with the two of them. That was why she came here, right?

"Snake, she's asking for a name and a way to contact the guy. She wants to see him again. Not have an all-night orgy. Carina needs to sit down and talk with him. Get to know him better." I narrowed my eyes. "You're aware that women sometimes want more than sex, right?"

"Sorry. I'm not just going to give her his information. We had a bit of fun once. Doesn't mean he'd be interested again."

I rolled my eyes. "You literally just said you'd call him to see if he wanted another threesome with her. So either he's interested or he's not. Is there a problem with calling him? Or are you just butt hurt she wants to talk to him and not you?"

Snake sneered at me and leaned in closer. "I may not be able to do anything about *you* being here, but I damn sure can kick her ass out."

Carina reached out to grab my hand. I felt the way she trembled and knew his words scared her. If she'd been caring for her girls on her own, and kept coming here, then she needed this place in order to survive. I couldn't let Snake kick her out.

"I know you don't like me, but don't punish Carina for it. She hasn't done anything wrong." I licked my lips. "Please, Snake. Let her stay."

"No. Both you bitches should leave since neither of you knows your place."

My heart lurched at the thought of leaving without Forge by my side. I saw Logan's expression when I turned to take a final sip of my watered-down drink and he gave me a reassuring nod. I had a feeling when I walked out the doors, someone would be waiting to walk me home. And if it was my fault Carina had been kicked out, then I'd be taking her with me. Damn Snake and everyone else. If they even tried to stop me, I'd kick them in the balls.

I gripped Carina's hand again and led her out the door. Kye waited at the bottom of the steps. He gave me a chin nudge and eyed Carina in curiosity. I hoped he didn't balk at her coming home with me.

"Come on. Kye will see we get to the house safely," I said.

"Um. I don't think Forge will want me in his house," Carina said.

"She's right, Whisper." Kye glanced at the clubhouse and back at me. "I know you've been gone a while, but this isn't the way things are done. Neither Forge nor Brick will like you taking her home with you."

"Well, Snake just kicked her out, and it's my fault. So she's coming with me whether the rest of you like it or not."

"My things are still inside," Carina said.

"I'll get them. Neither of you move," Kye said.

"Your usual spot?"

She nodded. We stood awkwardly while Kye ran inside. He came back holding a shirt and large bag. He handed both to Carina. She quickly pulled the shirt on and buttoned it before tying it at her waist. Her cheeks had a slight pink tinge to them, and I wondered if she was embarrassed about the situation. It probably wasn't every day an old lady saw her semi-dressed.

"I shouldn't go with you," Carina said.

"Maybe not, but you're going to. We need to figure out your situation. I screwed things up for you, so I'm going to fix it. And I won't take no for an answer."

Carina gave me a slight smile and a quick nod. "All right."

Kye drove us in one of the club vehicles and insisted on coming inside with us. He checked the house before giving the all clear. I didn't know if he expected the Boogeyman, or if he worried Tommy could have made his way into the compound. The thought had crossed my mind more than once.

"Are you staying too?" I asked Kye. He nodded and leaned against the wall near the front door.

"Come on, Carina. Let's go into the kitchen. I'll brew some tea and find us something to eat." We entered the kitchen and I checked to make sure Kye hadn't followed. "Do you need something for your girls for tonight?"

Carina only hesitated a moment before admitting she did.

"We need to come up with a long-term solution for you. Something that will keep you from having to visit the clubhouse every night. I'm not saying don't go if it's what you want, but I don't want you there because you feel you have no other options."

Carina sat on a kitchen chair and sagged, her body bowing as if a heavy weight had settled across her shoulders. In a way, I supposed it had.

"Where do you work?" I asked.

"The dollar store hired me part-time. I only work three hours some days and can get as many as five others. It's not enough to cover much of anything. My parents helped me once and only once. They gave me an old RV and paid the first four months at a campground. It's not perfect, but we have a bathroom, small kitchen, and a dry place to sleep."

"You can't get more hours?" I asked.

She shook her head. "The campground costs five hundred a month and that's only because they put us in a location no one else ever wants to rent. I didn't care as long I could keep my babies safe."

I might not have worked at a dollar store before, but I had a feeling she didn't make enough to cover the rent for her RV. I wasn't about to ask how she got the rest of the cash. It wasn't my business.

"Where are your girls right now?" I asked.

"A friend sits with them while I'm gone. She doesn't have anywhere else to go, so she's grateful for the use of the shower and some time out of the elements. She knows I'm struggling so she refuses to move in. Not that I have anywhere for her to sleep other than a crappy sofa."

"Did you drive here?" I asked.

"Yeah. My car isn't much to look at it. Rusted in more spots than I can count." She smiled. "I call it Trusty Rusty because it's been pretty reliable despite how ugly it is."

"And you have a fridge and way to cook at the RV?"

She nodded.

"I'm going to send a few things home with you,
and don't even think of saying no. It's for the girls.
They need to eat regular meals, and so do you. Spend
what time you can with them before trying to go back
to the clubhouse. I hate that you're there out of
obligation."

I heard a throat clear and saw Kye lounging in
the doorway. Crap! How much had he heard? The
concern on his face told me he'd heard more than I'd
have liked. I didn't know how Carina would react. I
could tell she was proud and hated that she couldn't
care for her children without getting help from others.

"Didn't mean to eavesdrop. That true, Carina?
You come here because you feel you have to?" he
asked.

Carina's eyes were wide, and she'd paled. I could
tell the thought of admitting such a thing terrified her.
I didn't think Kye would use it against her. If anything,
I thought he might want to help. Carina could use all
the people in her corner she could get. Even if Kye was
just a Prospect, he seemed like a good guy, and I
would trust him with Carina and her girls.

"What did you have in mind, Kye?" I asked.

"Not sure the club will like knowing she was
here under duress. They want the girls at the
clubhouse to enjoy partying. If they're here for
anything other than a good time, it tends to make the
men feel like they took advantage. Hell, Carina. I've
been with you several times since I got here and not
once did I ever realize you didn't really want to be
with me."

"Kye, no!" Carina shot to her feet. "It's not like
that."

"Then what?"

Carina twisted her hands in front of her, her

fingers laced together. She opened and shut her mouth, clearly not knowing what to say. The anguish and embarrassment etched on her features made my heart hurt for her.

"Kye, why don't you take a seat?" I asked. "I'll make you some coffee."

"I want to know what she meant." He crossed his arms, jaw set. I didn't think he asked out of anger. No, something else was going on and I had an idea as to what.

I walked over and placed my hand on his shoulder, giving him a nudge toward the table. "Sit!"

He took a seat across from Carina's spot and glowered at her. After the coffee had brewed, I poured him a cup and placed it in front of him before standing where I could view both him and Carina at the same time.

"Kye, are you worried you took advantage of Carina?"

He winced and grudgingly nodded.

"Carina, did you want to be with Kye the times the two of you were intimate?"

"Yes. I like Kye." She shot him a quick look before staring at her tea again. "He's nice to me and makes me feel beautiful. Some of the others just treat me like a convenience. With Kye it was different."

"You are beautiful," he murmured. "Figured you knew that."

"Here's what we're going to do," I said, clapping my hands to get their attention. "I'm going to put together a box of things to get you through a few days. Kye is going to follow you home when you leave, and you're going to make one stop. You're going to get some essentials like milk, eggs, and cheese at the store. I have some cash that should cover it, and don't even think to say no."

"Why does Kye need to go with me for that?" Carina asked.

"Because you're going to introduce him to your girls, make sure you have his number, and if an emergency comes up, I want you to call Kye. I think he'd be agreeable to that."

Kye nodded. "Absolutely. I didn't realize you had daughters. I'd love to meet them."

"You two get better acquainted while I get some food together." I went into the hall and pulled out one of the boxes I'd used to move in. Carrying it back to the kitchen, I loaded some canned goods into it, as well as unopened boxes of pancake mix, rice, and cereal. Then I took out a bag of frozen chicken breasts from the freezer and added it as well. It felt like there were six or seven in the package, so I hoped they'd get a few dinners out of it.

By the time I'd finished, Kye and Carina seemed closer and more at ease with one another. I hoped I'd given her another friend to rely on, and maybe something more. I saw the way Kye watched her. It seemed he had feelings for her. If I was right, then maybe things would be looking up for Carina soon enough. Kye didn't seem like the sort to hold her past against her. If she opened up and told him everything, I had a feeling he'd be her champion.

It felt good to help someone in need. And it made me wonder if there were other girls at the clubhouse in a similar situation. The club wouldn't be too happy if I ran off all the girls, and yet, I didn't want them to be there because they had no other options. It was wrong on so many levels, and I knew I needed to do something.

Chapter Eight

Forge

Shield paced the room while we waited on the others. Whatever he'd found out, it must be pretty fucking bad. I'd never seen him so rattled before. He kept glancing at the door and didn't sit until Beast, Hawk, and Prospero walked in. Since we still didn't have a club Secretary, we only had four officers at the moment.

"We have a problem," Shield said, bracing his hands on the back of a chair. He still hadn't sat, and it was starting to make me nervous.

"This have anything to do with Forge's woman?" Beast asked.

Shield held each of our gazes for a moment. "Tommy wasn't on any video footage because he didn't make it more than a mile away from the prison. His body was found in a shallow grave in the woods off the highway today."

"So Whisper can stop looking over her shoulder?" I asked. "Who the hell wanted that bastard dead besides us?"

"It seems Whisper wasn't the only girl Tommy raped. She's just the reason he got caught. I hacked into the prison's cameras and got a partial plate off the car picking up Tommy. When combined with the color, make, and model, it only came back with one possibility. Judge Wilcox."

"Why the hell would the judge pick him up?" Beast asked.

"I wondered the same thing. Went digging and discovered Wilcox has a stepdaughter. Two years ago, she was sent to a long-term care facility. Before that, she was in and out of treatment. Tommy and his friends did far worse to her than they did to Whisper. Girl was all torn up and beaten. She recovered physically, but mentally is another matter. Apparently the little shit covered his tracks enough they couldn't do anything legally, otherwise, he'd have never touched Whisper. He hurt that girl about six months before he attacked Whisper."

"How did you discover it was Tommy?" I asked.

"Found an email on the judge's personal account. He thought he deleted it, but I was able to access it still. He told the girl's biological father that Tommy wouldn't be a problem anymore."

"So the judge picked him up from the prison. Now Tommy's body has been found, and what? If anyone knew the judge was getting him, then the cops will go right to his door. The guy did us a favor far as I'm concerned. I don't want him to go to prison for it," I said.

"What do you recommend?"

"I think we need to either pay the judge a visit or have him come here." I leaned my elbows on the table. I knew the club wouldn't go for it, but I didn't think we needed to be seen going to the judge either.

"Here?" Beast asked. "Have you lost your fucking mind?"

"What if we arranged a meeting elsewhere? Neutral ground," Hawk said. "Shield could send an untraceable message to the judge. Something to lure him out."

"Where do you suggest we meet?" Beast asked.

"The property that backs up to ours is up for sale and currently vacant. I'll ask the judge to meet us in the old barn on the property," Shield said. "I think it's our safest bet. I'll check the area for cameras first and shut them all down before we head over there. What time do you want to do this?"

"Soon as possible," Beast said. "If we want to make sure the judge doesn't get arrested, then we need to talk to him immediately."

"I'll get it handled and message the four of you when I have it set up," Shield said.

Prospero tapped the table to get our attention. "Not that I don't want to show my support and all, but I sort of have plans that I can't cancel."

"What the fuck?" Beast growled. "Are you serious right now?"

"Look. I didn't want to say anything yet, but we're going to have another kid running around here soon. I found out last week I knocked up some girl a while back. She got arrested on drug charges and my kid was sent into foster care. The mom finally gave them my name and location and social services reached out. I have a meeting with the social worker, and I can't reschedule or I could lose the chance to get my kid." Prospero sighed. "I didn't want to say anything until I'd met with the woman today. There's a chance they'll not give my daughter to me."

"Anything I can do to help?" Shield asked.

"If I think of anything, I'll let you know. I want to try and do this the right way first. If that fails, then do your worst. I'm not letting my daughter get raised in a broken system that fails more kids than it saves." Prospero stood. "Sorry I can't be there this time."

"We need a club Secretary," I said. "It's past time."

"Well, we're all here right now. Anyone want to nominate someone?" Beast asked.

I looked over at Shield, but he was shaking his head. It seemed the hacker didn't want the job. There was only one other person I could think of who had been here long enough to have earned a spot as an officer. And I knew he was best friends with the President.

"What about Brick?" I asked.

"He didn't want a spot last time I asked him," Beast said.

"Ask again. What could it hurt?" I shrugged. "If he says no, then ask for other nominations, or during our next time in Church, see if anyone would be interested. The club has to vote either way."

"Everyone head home for now. Forge, I'm sure Whisper is ready to get out of the clubhouse. I saw she was talking to Carina." Hawk frowned. "You sure that's a good idea?"

"Whisper's an adult. If she wants to talk to Carina, I don't see the harm."

"Your funeral," Hawk said.

"I haven't slept with her. She won't be telling stories to Whisper about me. And if she does, Whisper already knows I have a past. I didn't lie to her. She's aware I've been with women since she's been gone."

"I'm heading home to my family," Beast said. "The rest of you can do whatever you want. Be ready to move when we get the call from Shield. I want this settled as quickly as possible."

I stood and walked out before anyone else lured me into conversation and froze the second I entered the main part of the clubhouse. Where the hell did Whisper go? I caught one of the club whores as she passed. Missy. At least, I thought that was her name. I hadn't ever been with her, but I'd seen her around plenty of times.

"You seen my wife?" I asked.

"Um." She danced from foot to foot and her gaze darted around. Shit. Something happened. "She left earlier."

"Why would she leave without me?" The girl looked ready to bolt. "Whatever happened, you need to tell me."

"Snake came. Your wife tried to get some information for Carina and Snake... He didn't treat her too well. Told her and Carina to leave."

I saw red. Literally. It felt like a haze settled over my vision as I stomped my way farther into the room, looking for that motherfucker. I knew he didn't like Whisper being back. I'd already had words with him, and I knew Brick had even gone after him with his fists.

The chickenshit bastard was gone. He'd probably decided to make himself scarce before I got out of Church and heard what he'd done. I'd deal with his ass later. Right now, I needed to make sure Whisper was all right. Since she'd come with me, I'd brought our new SUV. I'd ordered it online and had it delivered to the compound a few days ago. I'd wanted something that gave our family room to grow. While I loved Jacob, I wanted at least one or two more kids with Whisper.

I pulled into the driveway and home just in time to see Kye loading a box of food into the club truck and helping Carina into the vehicle. I had a feeling there was a story there, and Whisper had instigated it. Once Kye drove away, I went inside to find my wife. I'd have to tell her about Tommy, but first I needed to know what the hell she'd been up to and find out exactly what Snake had said or done. If I needed to beat on a brother, I wanted to get all the details first.

"Whisper!" I didn't see her in the living room and found her at the kitchen table, clearing away two mugs. "What's up with Kye and Carina?"

She smiled and put the mugs into the sink before giving me her full attention. "Carina is having a little trouble, so I thought I'd help. Before you get angry, I gave her some food... to make sure her daughters eat."

Well, fuck. I hadn't seen that one coming. "Daughters?"

She nodded. "If I tell you, can you keep it secret from the club? I think she's embarrassed."

I sighed and sat down. I had a feeling this talk wouldn't be short. "Go ahead. Unless it's going to harm the club in some way, I can keep a secret."

"She had a threesome with Snake and some random guy who isn't part of the club about four years ago. She got pregnant. One baby died but two little girls survived. They're three now. She showed me a picture, and there's no way Snake is the dad, so I tried to help her get the guy's information."

"And that's when Snake threw you and Carina out of the clubhouse?"

She winced. "Heard about that, did you? Pretty much. He's not my biggest fan. He refused to tell her anything, including the guy's name. So when we left, I brought her here. She goes to the clubhouse because someone in the kitchen gives her extra food to take home at the end of the night. She's barely making rent at the RV park and can't afford to feed her girls."

I didn't need or want to hear this. If Carina was only here in the hopes of feeding her girls, that meant she was whoring herself out to the club for food. It sickened me, and I knew my brothers wouldn't be too happy about it either. Were there others in the same situation? Shit. This was going to be a big clusterfuck.

"Why was Kye going with her?" I asked.

"He's taking her to her car, then he's going to make sure she gets a few essentials at the store like

Harley Wylde   Forge/ Naughty Or Nice

milk and eggs. He'll follow her home." She leaned back against the counter. "I think Kye likes her. He looked really upset when he thought she hadn't wanted to actually be with him. It seems they've gotten together a few times since he joined your club."

"So romance is in the air." I smiled. "He could do worse. Not sure he's ready to take on a ready-made family with two little girls, but maybe I'm wrong."

"It made me think... if Carina is having problems, then..."

"The others might not be here just because they like to party. Yeah, I was just thinking the same thing. Not sure how to bring that up to the club. Tonight isn't the time, though. Got some news from Shield about Tommy."

"Is he in the area?" she asked, going a little pale.

"No, angel. He's not. In fact, you never have to worry about him again. They found his body in the woods not too far from the prison. Looks like he wasn't out long before someone killed him. For the record, it wasn't any of us. We wouldn't have left him where he could be easily found. Clearly the guy is new at this. Fucker probably didn't even consider his car would be on camera."

"I like how you don't say you wouldn't have killed him. Only that you wouldn't have made it easy to get caught." She smiled. "It's a good thing I know you use those powers to help those who can't protect themselves."

"I may have to leave again shortly. I'm waiting on a call from Shield. He's setting up a meeting with the person who *did* kill Tommy. The guy wanted to avenge his stepdaughter. Tommy and his friends hurt her so bad she's in a mental care facility and may never get to leave there. We want to make sure the guy

- 106 -

doesn't go down for it."

"How are you going to do that?" she asked.

"Help him with an alibi, and a reason why his car would have picked up Tommy from prison. We don't know yet if anyone knew the guy was picking him up. If not, it will be easier to manipulate the situation." I stood and went to her, pulling her against me. "The man is a judge. If we can keep him out of jail, then maybe he'll do us a solid later. He's the sort of man we want on our side."

"Can I go with you? I want to thank him for what he did."

I wanted to tell her no, but something held me back. The judge might not like being surrounded by men from the club. Having Whisper there could work in our favor. Especially if he recognized her name. He wasn't the judge who'd overseen Tommy's trial, but it had been in all the local papers. We'd tried to keep Whisper's name out of it. Since she'd been in the video, and so many had seen it, we'd failed miserably.

"All right. The others may not like it, but I'll let you ride over there with me. We're meeting nearby."

"Does this mean after tonight it's over? No more Tommy? No more worrying about being safe when Jacob and I go somewhere?"

"That's what it means, baby."

She smiled so wide and so brightly any tension I'd held instantly melted away. Seeing her so happy felt like a miracle. Ever since the night Tommy and the other two attacked her, she'd not been fully living. Now she could put it behind her and truly move forward. I knew it would never go away completely. That night had shaped who she was today. But it didn't have to define her.

Chapter Nine

Whisper

I'd changed my clothes to meet with the judge. I'd wanted to look respectable. More than that, I knew I needed to soften the image of the Reckless Kings. The men standing with me were all rough. Each looked like a fierce warrior, and if I were the judge, I'd have turned tail and run. The man eyed each of them before setting his gaze on me. His expression softened.

"Judge Wilcox, my name is Whisper Woods. I'm married to the big guy behind me. Forge. But you may remember me as Whisper Evans. Seven years ago, Tommy and two other boys I'd graduated with drugged me, assaulted me, and filmed all of it before sending the video to our classmates."

"I remember," he said.

"I wanted to thank you. The Reckless Kings told me what you'd done, how you'd made sure Tommy didn't remain free for long. I've been so scared, constantly looking over my shoulder whenever I leave the house. You've given my life back to me. I can't tell you what it means to me, knowing that monster won't be free anymore."

The judge eyed the men again. "That why I'm here?"

"Not quite," Beast said. "You didn't do a good job of hiding the body or covering your tracks. If we found you, it's only a matter of time before the police come knocking at your door. Be thankful Shield hacked the cameras before the police got around to it. You know those fuckers move slower than molasses."

"We know what Tommy did to your stepdaughter," Hawk said. "We're sorry to hear about her condition, and we understand why you killed him.

In fact, we were planning to take care of the little shit once he surfaced."

"I need to know if anyone at the prison was aware you picked up Tommy," Shield said. "I tracked you using the camera footage at the prison and pulling a partial plate along with the make and model of your car. Which means anyone else could find that information too. I can erase that footage, but it won't do any good if someone knew you picked up Tommy."

The judge shook his head. "Didn't tell anyone. At least, no one who would say anything. How'd you know about my stepdaughter?"

"Email to her birth father. Deleting it didn't make it disappear. Not if you knew where to look," Shield said.

"So what now?" the judge asked.

"You need an alibi," I said. I might not know the judge, but I *did* know the Reckless Kings. The club wouldn't be helping this man if he was a bad guy. "We don't want you to go to prison for killing Tommy. It wouldn't be fair. You've upheld the law until now, haven't you? It's your job, and I'd like to think you wouldn't have gotten the position if you hadn't earned it, as well as the respect of the town citizens. I've seen your name in the paper, attending charity events or visiting sick kids in the hospital. You do so much good, and he was rotten to the core. If he'd remained free, it would only have been a matter of time before he attacked someone else."

"Why would you help me?" Judge Wilcox asked. "We aren't exactly on the same side."

"I think you're wrong," I said. "These men may not always follow the law, but they're good guys. They help women and children. Did you know one of them adopted me? The man I later married is the one who found me. He saved me from a rapist who'd kidnapped me. When the club discovered my family had died, Brick decided to keep me as his daughter."

"That's just one thing," the judge said.

I nodded. "It is. One of them is off helping a single mom right now. He's helping her get groceries and making sure her two little girls have food for the next week, and I know he'll keep an eye on them in the future in case they need anything else. They've left to help other clubs when they've tried to rescue women in trouble. They've taken care of rapists, pedophiles, and so many others who slipped through the cracks in the justice system. Are you going to condemn them for doing the same thing you did?"

The judge looked away and seemed to shrink in on himself. He might not have liked what I had to say, but I hoped it would help him see reason. It took a few minutes before the man seemed to come to a decision. He stood a little straighter and met the gaze of each man standing with me.

"All right. Tell me what we need to do," he said.

While the men came up with an alibi for the judge, and had him go over the story multiple times, I checked out the barn and surrounding area. It looked like whoever had owned this property had kept horses at one point. An old saddle remained in the tack room, the leather dried out and brittle. I found a momma cat with a litter of kittens in the back stall. She hissed and growled at me, so I backed off, giving them space.

Oddly, the place gave a feeling of home, even though I'd never lived anywhere like it before. I didn't know if it was the structure, so much as the overall vibe the place gave off. Or maybe it was the cat with her kittens. I'd never had a pet. Dad probably would have gotten me one if I'd asked. Then when I'd been on my own, I couldn't afford to take care of one. Jacob would probably love a kitten or puppy. I'd have to talk to Forge about it.

By the time they'd finished their conversation, I was more than ready to go home. I didn't know if my dad would keep Jacob all night, and I didn't want to be gone if my son wanted to come home. Although, he'd settled into his new life with ease. He adored getting to see his grandpa whenever he wanted, and he loved spending time with Forge.

"Want to get dinner out before we head home?" Forge asked, taking my hand and leading me out to the SUV.

"What about Jacob?"

"Brick texted me earlier. Jacob wants to spend the night and I told him that was fine. I didn't know how tired you'd be, and honestly, I like having you all to myself sometimes. I love Jacob. I'm not saying I don't. But…"

"We haven't had a lot of *us* time."

He nodded. "Right."

"Dinner, then home. I'm not sleepy, but I do want to get comfortable."

He leaned in closer, kissing me senseless. "When we get home, we're going to celebrate."

I buckled my seat belt as he walked around to the driver's side and got in. I couldn't help but smile. There was no doubt in my mind exactly what Forge was thinking.

Most of the restaurants in town had full parking lots, which meant we'd have to wait at least twenty minutes if not longer. Forge passed one after another, until he gave up and parked outside the diner. It might not be the most glamorous place to eat, but I'd missed the diner while I'd been gone. When I'd lived here before, I'd eaten at this place a lot. Not only with Dad, but with my friends and even with Forge.

We went inside and took a seat at a booth by the window. One of the servers hurried over and gave us a tired smile. I blinked when I realized I'd gone to school with her. Nerves hit me and I wondered if she'd recognize me. I hadn't seen anyone from my high school since the field party after graduation. I'd known I'd run into some of them eventually. It wasn't like our town was all that large. I just hadn't been prepared to do it tonight.

"What can I get..." She froze and her eyes went wide. She glanced at Forge and back at me. "Um..."

"Problem?" Forge asked.

She shook her head. "No, sorry. It's good to see you, Whisper."

I felt Forge tense next to me and knew he'd realized this woman had known me when I'd lived here before. It seemed I wasn't the only one taken by surprise. I placed my hand on his thigh and gave it a squeeze, letting him know I was all right.

"Good to see you too, Melanie. I'll have a sweet tea, please."

"Coffee," Forge said. "And a glass of water."

She nodded and rushed off, glancing at us over her shoulder. I wondered how long before she told all her friends I was back in town. Or had she even kept up with anyone we'd gone to school with?

"Should we leave?" Forge asked, his voice low so only I could hear him.

"It's fine. It would be unreasonable to run every time I see someone I went to school with. Better to get it over with."

Forge put his arm around my shoulders and hugged me tight to his side. I hadn't expected him to slide into the booth beside me. When I'd sat, I'd thought for sure he'd sit across the table. I didn't mind him being beside me. If anything, it made me feel safer. More settled. I knew that if anyone wanted to hurt me, verbally or physically, they'd have to go through Forge first. And no one was getting past him.

Melanie came back with our drinks and set them on the table. We ordered our food and I tried to ignore the looks she kept giving me. We hadn't been close in high school. If we had, I might have volunteered a bit of information. Like where I'd been the last seven years, how I was doing, why I was back... Instead, I kept quiet.

Forge leaned in a little after she walked off and spoke low. "Should we just submit an article to the local newspaper? You know everyone in here, the ones who recognize you, are all wondering the same thing."

"How I landed such a handsome, fantastic guy like you?"

He narrowed his eyes at me. "Smartass. You'll pay for that when we get home."

I pressed my thighs together. I could think of worse fates. Now I'd be wet and aching the rest of dinner, while I fantasized about all the ways he might punish me. We hadn't gotten too crazy in the bedroom. Other than him pinning me down, the occasional smack on my ass, things had been fairly vanilla. Would that change tonight?

"I wish I could make everything right," Forge said. "I don't like people staring at you or whispering. They don't have any idea what you've been through, what you've survived." He winced. "Unless they saw the video. The newspaper ran an article, but they left out a lot of details."

"It's fine, Forge."

"It's not," he grumbled.

Well, no, it wasn't. Didn't suddenly make things different. People would talk and stare. It's what they did. Sooner or later, they'd get bored and move on to another topic. Once I wasn't the shiny new bit of gossip, they'd treat me like anyone else in this town.

Our food arrived and we ate quickly. Our date had lost some of its shine. I didn't like feeling as if I were a zoo exhibit. Forge paid the ticket and we left. He hadn't received any calls or texts about Jacob, so I assumed our little one was having fun with his grandpa. With some luck, he'd stay there past breakfast.

The house was dark when we pulled into the driveway. Forge helped me from the SUV and we went inside. He flipped on the entry light and took me by the hand, leading me toward the bedroom. He stopped at the hall closet and reached up on the top shelf, taking down a small box. I had no idea what it was inside, or where it had come from, but it seemed I was going to find out soon.

Forge nudged open the bedroom door with his foot and stepped inside, pulling me in his wake. We had the house to ourselves, which meant we didn't have to lock the door, or listen for Jacob in case he woke. Forge put the box on the bed and jerked his chin toward the bathroom.

"Go rinse off and I'll get things ready in here. I'll join you in a minute."

"I don't want to see the water bill. Every time I turn around, you're shoving me into the shower or telling me to get in the tub. I'm going to get a complex and think I stink."

He grinned. "Maybe I just want you nice and relaxed."

I stared at him. I could see that being part of his reasoning. There had to be more to it, though. "You like seeing me all wet and naked, don't you?"

"I'll never tell."

I rolled my eyes and went into the bathroom. I stripped my clothes off and started the shower. The hair clip on the counter caught my attention and I used it to pull my hair up. After the water was the right temperature, I stepped under the spray. The water pounded my neck and shoulders, and I had to admit it felt nice.

I heard Forge making noise in the other room. I didn't know what he was up to, but I couldn't wait to find out. Our night hadn't gone quite as planned. At least, the dinner out hadn't. If only Melanie hadn't made things so weird. The moment she'd said my name, other people close enough to hear had started to gossip.

I felt Forge's hands land on my hips, and I leaned back against him. He took his time washing me. The way his hands glided over my skin made me shiver. Being with Forge felt more amazing than anything I'd experienced before. Each time, it felt even better than the last.

"I'm the luckiest bastard," he murmured, kissing the side of my neck. "I have the sexiest wife in the world, a smart kid... Can't think of much else I need to be happy."

I took his hand and placed it over my belly. "Maybe one more thing. We don't have a daughter yet."

"Guess we'd better get to work on that, then. Can't have you telling people I haven't given you everything you need."

"Do I get to see the surprise in the bedroom

now?"

He nipped my shoulder. "You sound excited about it. What if it's something you end up hating?"

"We'll never know if you don't show me."

Forge shut off the water and dried us both quickly before taking my hand and leading me into the bedroom. I gasped when I saw he'd used candles to light the room. Ropes hung from the headboard and seemed to be strung under the mattress at the foot of the bed. He'd laid a satin blindfold on my pillow, and I saw a few different toys on the nightstand, as well as a bottle of lube.

"Too much?" he asked.

"No. At least, I don't think so." I took it all in again. "If I end up feeling overwhelmed, I'll let you know. But I trust you, Forge."

He cupped my cheek and pressed his forehead to mine. "Can't use my name right now?"

I smiled. "Victor."

"There we go. That wasn't so hard, was it?"

I reached down to place my hand over his hard cock. "No, but you are."

He closed his eyes and laughed silently. I felt his body shaking as he pulled away. "Cute. Get on the bed, angel. On your back."

I did as he commanded, placing my hands by the headboard. He knelt on the side of the bed and picked up the blindfold, tying it over my eyes. I felt his hands on my wrists and then the ropes going around them. I tugged when he'd finished and realized he hadn't tied me tight enough for it to hurt, but I wouldn't be escaping either. Forge grasped my ankle and pulled my leg until I'd spread my thighs. He tied one leg, then the other, leaving me open and vulnerable.

My heart pounded against my ribs. I trusted him,

more than anyone else. If I didn't, I'd have been freaking out by now. While I didn't remember anything that happened at the field party, something like this would have triggered a panic attack if it had been with some random guy. I'd known Forge since I'd been fifteen. He'd saved me more than once, and I knew he'd never do anything to hurt me.

Still, I felt a little apprehensive. Not being able to see what he was doing did give me a certain thrill, and yet, I felt my muscles tense. Forge ran his fingers lightly down my thigh before leaning over me. His lips brushed mine and any tension melted.

"Victor," I said, his name nearly a whisper.

"Trust me, baby?"

"You know I do. I'm just... I've never done anything like this before." I bit my lip. "It won't hurt, will it?"

"Whisper, I told you. I won't ever do anything to hurt you. That includes in the bedroom. If something *does* hurt, you tell me. This is supposed to be fun, to feel good. If it doesn't, I need to know."

"All right."

"We don't have to try all this stuff tonight. I'll pick one thing and see how you like it. I'll take my cues from you, baby."

"I'm ready, Victor." I heard the whirr of something and gave a little shriek when I felt it touch my nipple. The plastic felt cool against my skin, but the buzzing soon felt incredibly good. I moaned and strained against the ropes. "Oh, God! It feels... feels..."

He switched to the other side, making me whine. I felt myself getting wetter, and an ache started to build. I needed him! Wanted him. What he was doing felt good, but it wasn't enough.

"That's it. Beg me for it. Tell me what you want."

"Make me come, Victor. Please."

He slid the toy down my body, not stopping until he'd spread my pussy open. I felt the buzzing against my clit and my body arched as I started to come. I'd never felt anything so intense. I cried out, screaming his name. Pleasure coursed through me, and I never wanted it to end.

"More?" he asked.

I nodded frantically, unable to say anything else. My tongue felt heavy, and I couldn't form words. One orgasm rolled into another, then another. My entire body felt electrified. I sobbed when he took the toy away. Forge released the ropes from around my ankles, then my wrists. I thought he was finished with me, but I was wrong.

He flipped me onto my stomach and started tying me up again. He worked his hand between my lower belly and the bed, and I felt the toy pressing against me. Forge positioned it against my clit, and I wanted to cry it felt so wonderful.

"That's it, baby. Keep coming."

His weight settled over me and he slowly pressed his cock into me, stretching me open. He rocked against me, working himself in deeper. Between the fullness, and the stimulation, I felt like I was on overload. I came multiple times as he fucked me.

By the time he'd finished, and I was able to catch my breath, I knew he'd just broken me. No man would ever satisfy me the way he had. Not that I'd ever wanted to leave him. No, Forge was my other half, the man I'd always wanted. I loved him, even if it terrified me to say the words. He'd said he couldn't love me, and now it was the one thing I wanted most. Even more than a daughter.

Forge untied me and removed the blindfold. While he cleaned up the toy he'd used, I snuggled under the covers. As much as I wanted to clean up, I felt boneless and didn't want to move. He came back to bed and slid in next to me. I curled against him and breathed in his scent.

"So that's a yes on the blindfold, being tied up, and at least one of the toys," he said.

"If you couldn't tell for sure, I'm going to have to rethink this marriage. I thought you were smart. Now I'm questioning my belief in you."

He smacked my ass and I yelped. "Watch it, baby girl. We haven't checked to see if you like spankings yet. I will gladly turn your ass red."

Now why did the idea of that turn me on? It seemed Forge was corrupting me. And I was gladly going to let him.

Chapter Ten

Forge

Some guys learn the hard way. Apparently I'm one of them. I learned not to ignore Whisper's concerns about security -- or anything else -- when things blew up about two weeks later. Both figuratively and literally -- Carina's RV exploded. No way that was an accident.

Kye managed to pull Clover back at the last second. Both were blasted off their feet, and poor little Clover took the brunt of the debris and heat. Her face and parts of her body had not only been burned but had also been cut by flying pieces of metal. Carina and Poppy hadn't made it.

As the Sergeant-at-Arms, I should have seen this shit coming. And Whisper had brought up helping the girls more than once. It proved one thing... those women were practically invisible to me and everyone else in the club. Except, apparently, my wife.

We didn't know who was responsible yet, but I would damn well find out. And there would be hell to pay when I did. The more we sifted through the remains of their home, the more I discovered. Like pieces of notes Carina had apparently received. Or rather, threats. Someone hadn't been happy my wife had helped out Carina and her girls, and they'd hated the fact Kye had taken an interest in the family. At least, that's what I'd pieced together from what I'd found. The charred pieces of paper had blown free during the explosion, even though some had been too badly charred to make sense of them.

If it hadn't been for the favor the judge owed us, we wouldn't have had the opportunity to look through any of it. He managed to stall the police with one of his long-winded speeches long enough to give us a head start.

"Kye at the hospital?" Beast asked as he took a seat. I'd come into Church so I could spread the evidence out and try to make heads or tails of all this shit.

"Yeah. He's staying with Clover for now. Wants to make sure she's stable." I moved a few bits around again, hoping something would fit together like a damn jigsaw puzzle.

"Not to add to your apparent stress level right now, but any idea what's going to happen to that girl?" Beast asked.

Shit. I sighed and hung my head. I hadn't even considered it. If Carina had been in dire straits, it meant there likely wasn't family to take the girl in. I didn't like the thought of her entering the foster system. Sometimes they got it right, and other times it went horribly wrong. Brick had kept Whisper from suffering that fate. I hoped someone here would step up and do the same for Clover.

"I'll call Kye," Beast said. "I'll give him first option."

"On what? Keeping Clover?"

He nodded. "Little girl needs someone in her corner. Seems like Kye has been there for the last two weeks. He's gotten to know her, clearly cares about her. If he doesn't want the responsibility, I'll check with our brothers before reaching out to the other clubs. I know Havoc and Jordan at the Devil's Boneyard have adopted some kids. They may take on another. If not, there's always Grizzly, although he's gotten up there in years. Might not want to take on someone as young as Clover."

We'd all known why he'd decided to spend time

with the ex-club whore and her kids. Aside from the fact he'd had a crush on her since the first time he saw her, once Kye found out she needed help, he'd wanted to be her hero. I hoped he'd given her some peace the last two weeks, and possibly given her a reason to smile. Despite the fact we'd known what he was doing, it hadn't really triggered a response in any of us to check on the other women. It should have, but I'd be the first to admit I'd been too focused on my own family. I didn't doubt for a second the others hadn't given those women a thought either, unless they wanted to get their dick sucked.

"Let me know how it goes. I'm sure Whisper will ask."

"You need anything from me right now?"

I shook my head and moved the pieces around again. I glance at the bits I'd found of what I'd determined to be the explosive device. The cops had been called in, so I'd had to pocket what I could before they arrived. It worked in our favor that this particular RV park wasn't in the best area of town. People weren't as likely to ask the cops to come around. The fire department, perhaps, but since there were no flames, I didn't think they'd be in a rush to get there. Someone had definitely called the police, though, and it meant we'd had limited time to go through the debris ourselves. The device had seemed to be crudely made, which led me to believe an amateur had put it together. Hell, they might have even run a damn Google search to figure out how to build the fucking thing.

Something felt really off about the entire thing. Who would want to hurt Carina and two children? As far as I knew, she didn't have enemies. The only time I'd heard of anyone even raising their voice to her, or treating her badly, had been the conversation she and Whisper had with Snake the night my wife met her. I didn't see Snake doing something like this, and if he had, it wouldn't have been such a shitty job.

As if I'd conjured him with my thoughts, he walked through the doors and stopped before he got close to the table or me. He scanned the items and fisted his hands at his sides. "I want to help."

"What? You aren't relieved she's gone?" I asked. Yeah, it made me an asshole, but I was tired and pissed as fuck about the situation.

"I might not have wanted her hanging around the clubhouse anymore, but it didn't mean I wanted her dead. And I sure the fuck didn't want any kids to die."

I waved him off. "Fine. You want to help? Give me your ideas on who would want to hurt Carina and her kids. Because right now, I can't think of one fucking person."

"Anyone know who the father is?" Snake asked. "Maybe he didn't like Kye hanging around them so much."

I hadn't wanted to bring it up with Snake. Whisper claimed he knew the father and had refused to give Carina the man's information. Which meant Snake likely didn't know who the girls belonged to. I wasn't sure how he'd take the news, but I didn't have anything else to go on.

"You'd have to tell me about the dad."

Snake's brow furrowed and he crossed his arms. "Why the hell would I know?"

"Because she apparently got pregnant the night you and your friend had a threesome with Carina. Since the girls don't look anything like you, I'm going to assume they belong to the other guy."

Snake staggered back a step. "What the fuck? Are you shitting me? Did that slut say that? No. No fucking way."

"She told Whisper the next morning she realized one of the condoms must have broken. She was sticky with cum. So one of you is the father. If you're saying it's not your friend, does that mean you're stepping up as daddy?"

Snake started to pace. "This can't be happening."

"Beast is checking with Kye to see if he wants to adopt Clover," I said. "So you're both off the hook as far as that goes. But if you really believe the girls' father would have set that bomb…"

Snake shook his head. "No. He'd never do something like that. If he'd known about the girls, he'd have run as far as he could, but he wouldn't have tried to kill them, or Carina."

"Are you going to tell him about Clover?" I asked.

"No. Trust me. He's the last person you want raising that little girl. If Kye wants her, let him have her. At least he's familiar to Clover."

"Doesn't solve the mystery of who the hell blew them up." I backed away from the table and ran my hand over my face. "I never heard of any trouble with Carina here at the clubhouse. Did anyone hate her? Hold a grudge?"

The doors opened again, and my wife poked her head into the room. "Can I come in?"

"No pussy allowed in Church," Snake said.

I didn't even hesitate. I walked over to Snake and broke his fucking nose. The asshole glared as he tipped his head back and pinched the bridge. "Motherfucker, don't talk to my wife like that."

Whisper came farther into the room, and I

hugged her to me. "I'm sorry. I wasn't trying to cause trouble. But I had an idea."

"What's that?" I asked.

"When I walked in just now, there were a few women in the clubhouse. Including the one who tried to start trouble the night you brought me here for a drink. Paris? I think that's her name. Tall woman who didn't want to keep her hands to herself."

I nodded and waited to see what else she had to say. But if that bitch had done something to my woman, or said something, I was going to drag her ass out of here by her fucking hair, and I didn't give a shit if she had clothes on or not.

"She sneered at me and said a few nasty things. I think she's angry I befriended Carina and tried to help her."

Snake stalked through the doors into the hall. "I'm assuming Church is just open to anyone right now. Unless you want to interview the women in one of the bedrooms?"

"Fuck no! I don't want them getting the wrong idea."

"I'll send someone in with her. I need to try and set my fucking nose," Snake said.

I flipped him off behind Whisper's back. I hoped it didn't heal straight. It would serve him right. No way I would sit back and let him insult my wife. Sooner or later, Snake and I were going to have it out. His problems with Whisper were petty and needed to end.

Satyr dragged Paris through the doors and shoved her down into a chair. The bitch snarled at him like a feral dog and my fingers itched to knock some sense into her. I'd never been one to hurt a woman, but right now she was a suspect and someone who didn't like my wife. Since Whisper outranked her, she needed to learn her fucking place, or she could leave and not come back.

"I hear you have an issue with my wife," I said.

Paris glared at Whisper before smiling at me. "Did you decide to take me up on my offer?"

"Why do you hate Whisper?"

Paris' expression blanked. She looked from my wife to me and settled back in her chair. She relaxed her posture, but I could see the tension in her muscles. For some reason, she wanted me to think she didn't have a care in the world.

"What was so special about Carina?" Paris asked.

"She needed help." Whisper wrapped her fingers around my bicep before leaning closer to me. "She confided she only came here as a way to get food for her girls. When I heard where she was living, and how those babies were starving, I did what I could to help her out. No one should sell themselves for any reason, unless they just want to."

"Whisper talked to me later that night. She told me if Carina had been coming here because she felt she had no other options, then some of the women might be doing the same thing. I didn't get a chance to look into it because of other shit going on with the club and my family. So is that why you hate her? Are you here because you feel there's nowhere else for you to go?" I asked.

Paris blinked and looked away. "Not everyone gets to have a fairy-tale ending."

"Who had the fairy tale?" Whisper asked. "Me? Carina?"

Paris nodded. "I heard about you. Snake hasn't shut up about you turning your back on the club, walking away. You went through a trauma and instead of letting them help, you ran. Then Forge brings you here. He *married you* so no one could toss you out. One conversation with Carina, and suddenly you're her best friend. She stopped coming here because she didn't need to anymore. You gave her food for her kids and sent Kye to help her."

"Not quite. I noticed the way Kye watched her. I wouldn't have forced him to help her. He did it because he cared about her, and I think he cared about those girls too. And now Carina and Poppy are dead."

Paris' eyes went wide. "What? What the hell are you talking about?"

"Someone set off a bomb at Carina's RV today. She and Poppy died in the blast. Little Clover is at the hospital, but I'm not sure if she'll make it. If she does, she has no family to look after her." I watched Paris, wondering if this was an act, or if she genuinely hadn't known. When Whisper had mentioned Paris's reaction to her today, I'd had a brief moment where I'd considered Paris might have harmed Carina.

Tears filled Paris's eyes and she openly cried. "Oh, God! I'm sorry. I didn't have any idea. Poor Carina! And those girls…"

"Can you think of anyone who might have wanted to hurt Carina?" Whisper asked. "Did the two of you ever talk? Maybe she mentioned something in passing that could help the club find who did this to her."

Paris shook her head. "No. I mean some of the girls can be catty, myself included, but I don't think any of them would have hurt her, and definitely not her children. We were jealous over her good fortune when you decided to help her. Even then, I wouldn't have done anything to her."

Whisper tugged on my arm. "Forge, maybe you

need to talk to the girls one on one. See if any of them seems to be hiding something."

"I hate to think a woman could do something like this, but you're right. I can't rule it out. Hell, I wondered for a moment if Paris could have done it." Paris made a squeaking sound and tensed. "Calm down. I don't think that anymore. But I do have a question for you. If you aren't here because you like to party, why do you come to the clubhouse?"

She dropped her gaze to the floor. "Because I don't have anywhere else to go. If I'm lucky, someone will let me stay the night with them, or at least not kick me out of the clubhouse overnight. It's safer to sleep here than on the streets."

"Told you," Whisper said softly, nudging me.

Shit. Yeah, she'd called it. The club had a bunch of women who were hiding from the world or trying to better their situation, and they were spreading their legs for my brothers in order to get what they needed. I fucking hated it, and I knew the others would too. Seemed like we needed to clean house. I wouldn't just toss them all out, though. No, we'd have to figure out how to help them, and make sure in the future that all women who came to party were here for the right reasons. "There's an empty room down the hall. I'll send Logan out to get some bunk beds. Might be a tight squeeze, but it would give four of you a place to sleep if you need it. It's not a permanent solution, but it might work for now."

Whisper leaned up and kissed my cheek. "I'm going to help him. They'll need more than just the beds. I doubt he'll think about mattresses, bedding, you'll have to have space for them to store their clothes, and the bathroom will need to be stocked with things a woman might require."

I placed my finger over her lips. "I get it. You're better equipped for this task than a man. Go help Logan. Tell him exactly what I said I wanted, and that you have free rein for how the task is carried out. If you go with him, make sure you take someone else too. See if Crow is available."

"Be nice to them, Forge. Until you know for sure one of them killed Carina and Poppy, you need to treat them like women you want to help. Because we *will* help them. Right?"

I sighed and nodded. "Yeah, angel. We're going to help them. Now go get started on that room. It's going to take a few hours to get it all set up."

"Can I help?" Paris asked softly.

"The room hasn't been used in a while. Probably needs a good scrubbing. Same for the bathroom. Think you can handle that?"

"It's going to be for me to use?" she asked. "And anyone else who needs a place to crash?"

"Yeah, it will be."

"Then I'll gladly clean it." Paris stood.

"Send Missy in here." I had a feeling it was going to be a long fucking day. It took hours to interview all the women present, and I sent my brothers out after the ones unaccounted for. They brought back all but one. Flossie hadn't been at home, or anywhere else around town that Shield had noticed. He'd tried to use the town's cameras to track her with no luck, but he'd found something disturbing.

Flossie might not have been in town right now, but she'd been around earlier. In fact, a traffic camera had caught her heading right for the RV park about an hour before Carina had gone home with the girls. I had a feeling we'd just found the person responsible.

Now we had to find the bitch.

Chapter Eleven

Whisper

I couldn't have been prouder of Forge, or the Reckless Kings. I knew they'd helped people before. Heck, I'd been one of them. But this was different. They hadn't realized the women right under their roof had needed their help, and now that they did, Forge was doing what he could to make their lives better.

Giving them beds at the clubhouse would work for right now wasn't a long-term solution. However, it bought everyone time to figure out something else. Like finding the women jobs and helping them find places of their own. I wanted to be a part of it and do what I could. If Forge hadn't brought me home with him that day, if Brick hadn't adopted me, I might very well have ended up in a similar situation.

Logan had found a store that not only carried bunk beds and other basic bedroom essentials, but they also stocked sheets and pillows. We loaded up one of the club trucks with two bunk beds, two five-drawer chests, and bedding. Then I'd found the section for bathroom items and bought a bath mat, towels, shower gel, and other things I thought the women might need.

I didn't know what their clothing situation might be, so I talked Logan into letting me pick up a few pair of leggings and some long-sleeved tunics in each size. It wasn't perfect, but if they didn't have enough clothing, it would at least give them something extra. Once I knew who would be staying in the room, I could better assess their needs. Assuming Forge would let me. I knew it wasn't normal for the wives or old ladies to talk to the club whores, much less take a hands-on approach to helping them.

We hauled everything back to the clubhouse.

While Logan and two other men put the bunk beds together, as well as the two chests, I met with the women who would be using the space. In addition to Paris, there were two others... Yasmin and Gypsy. I had no idea if those were their real names, but it's how they'd introduced themselves.

"Why are you helping us?" Gypsy asked.

"Because it's the right thing to do," I said. "I have no issue with women who want to come here and have some fun. What I don't like is the fact you felt you had no other options. I could have been in your shoes. If Brick hadn't adopted me, then who knows what I'd have done in order to survive?"

"Brick is your daddy?" Yasmin's eyes went wide. "Holy shit."

"No wonder Forge married you," Paris said. "Despite what happened to you, the fact Brick claimed you as his kid made you part of the club. I know you walked out, but they'd have stood by you if you hadn't."

Maybe it should have surprised me that they knew what I'd been through. Then again, after living around bikers for a decade, I knew they gossiped worse than little old ladies. One or two, if not more, had probably been running their mouths in the clubhouse and the girls had overheard.

I nodded. "I know. Back then, I was so embarrassed and ashamed of what had happened that I ran. I didn't want to look at these men and see the pity in their eyes. Especially Forge. He's one of the ones who found me."

"You really think this is going to make a difference for us?" Gypsy asked.

"You're going to have a place to sleep, no strings attached. If you don't want to party with the men anymore, you don't have to. I made sure the bathroom will be stocked with anything you could need. And since I didn't know what your clothing situation would be, I did pick up some leggings and shirts in different sizes." I met each of their gazes. "Please don't be ashamed to ask for help. If you need something, either tell one of the guys or tell me. I'll leave my number with you."

Gypsy looked away before reluctantly turning back toward me. "I don't have anything but what I'm wearing and two dresses that wouldn't be appropriate for finding a job."

"Write down your sizes and I can get you a few things, or if you'd prefer to shop for yourself, I can ask one of the Prospects to take you shopping." I leaned back in my chair. "Same for all of you. I want you to have the tools you need to succeed."

"You going to help us get jobs too?" Yasmin asked.

"The club is going to check around and see what's available. They'll provide you with a list, as well as applications if those places have paper ones. Most companies have gone the electronic route. In which case, you'll be given access to a computer so you can apply for whichever jobs you want."

"This seems too good to be true," Paris said. "I wanted to hate you, but I can't. Not when you're doing all this for us."

"Once you have a job, you'll be able to save up some money. The club isn't going to throw you out. I want you to feel secure in your jobs and feel comfortable being on your own. Or maybe the three of you could find a place to rent together. Entirely up to you."

Gypsy traced a pattern on the table with her

finger. "I wouldn't know what would be appropriate for job interviews and stuff like that. Could you get some stuff for me?"

I nodded. "I'd be happy to. Just write down your sizes and any color preferences. Be sure to include shoe size."

"Would you help us with our hair and makeup?" Paris asked. "So we can look more respectable like you? New clothes won't matter if people see us and still think we look like whores."

"I'll help in whatever way I can, and however you'll let me. I don't want you to feel like I'm forcing myself on you. Any of you. I'm here if you need me, but otherwise, I'll let you handle things on your own." I smiled at the three of them. "I know it's unusual for me to be sitting here with you. Your first instinct is probably to lash out or hate me just because I'm married to Forge. And I get it. I'm a threat to you, or I was. Women who come here to party don't like it when the guys settle down. It's one less man for them to enjoy, or to try and claim for their own."

"You're different," Paris said. "We've never met anyone like you before. Carina was right. You treated us with respect that day. I'm sorry for the way I acted."

"It's all right, Paris. You had your reasons."

"Furniture is together, Whisper," Logan said as he stepped out of the hallway and into the main room. "Need anything else?"

"Not right now. Thank you, Logan. All right, ladies. Let's get the sheets and blankets on the beds. I'll let you each do your own, and I'll start on the bathroom. Logan told me there's only a standing shower in there, so I didn't need a shower curtain, but I did get a bath mat and some towels for you. There are also new toothbrushes, toothpaste, tampons, and other stuff I thought you might need."

The women eagerly went to the bedroom and picked the beds they wanted. Paris ended up on the bottom bunk of one bed, while Yasmin and Gypsy decided to sleep in the other bunk bed, with Gypsy taking the top. By the time they finished putting the bedding on their chosen beds, I'd finished with the bathroom. There wasn't a lot of storage space, or counter space for that matter, so I knew it would be cramped. Hopefully, they wouldn't end up fighting with each other. I knew the close quarters could prove problematic over time.

Forge found me a short while later. I could tell right off something was wrong. He looked like someone had placed a heavy weight on him. Which meant he likely had found the person responsible for killing Carina and Poppy, or at least had his suspicions. I'd kept in touch with Kye via text throughout the day, and there hadn't been any change with Clover. I didn't know if her waking would be a good thing or not. Would she be in a lot of pain when she did come to?

"I asked Brick to keep Jacob. With everything going on, I didn't think you'd be up to taking care of him tonight. You have to be worn out."

"I am." I ran my hand up and down his back. "You all right?"

"No. We've discovered who set the bomb. It's one of the girls. Except she's apparently run. Shield is going to ask Wire and a few others to help track her down, but it's possible we'll never find her."

"Is Kye going to keep Clover?"

"He asked Shield to work a little computer magic. Kind of like he did with Jacob. Clover will be coming home with Kye, except... he doesn't have a home. Prospects usually don't have a family, so we don't give them houses."

"Then we should get a place ready for him and Clover," I said. "Are there any empty ones right now?"

Forge nodded. "One. It's small. Might be okay for just him and Clover, though."

"Furnished?"

"No. The club will cover the cost of the basics. And whatever Clover will need. But right now, I'm tired as fuck. I just want to go home and crawl into bed with you."

"We need food, Forge. You haven't eaten since this morning."

"Later." He kissed my forehead. "I need to rest a bit first."

"Want me to drive us home?"

"I've got it, angel."

I took his hand and walked out to our SUV. The drive home was quiet, and I had to admit he'd been right. It had been a long day, and I was every bit as tired as him. When we pulled into the driveway, I didn't even want to get out. I hadn't realized I was exhausted until I thought about having to go into the house.

"Your adrenaline is crashing," Forge said. "Mine too. We're probably going to sleep for hours."

"I'm okay with that. As long as no one needs us. Think we'll hear the phone if it goes off?"

"Yeah. It will wake me up."

I managed to get out and go into the house. My feet were dragging as I went back to the bedroom. I didn't even bother changing out of my clothes. I kicked my shoes off and collapsed onto the bed, then crawled up far enough to reach my pillow. I felt the bed dip as Forge got in next to me, then I was in his arms.

"Night, my beautiful, kind, and perfect wife," he murmured.

I tried to respond, but sleep pulled me under.

Chapter Twelve

Forge
Two months later

It had been a while since I'd been able to work on any new projects. The clang of my hammer pounding the metal over the anvil made my soul sing. I'd earned my name for good reason. This was the place where I felt most settled, where the rest of the world melted away. When things went to shit, I created something new. Sometimes those things were beautiful, and other times they were what some would call scary.

This particular item would definitely qualify as beautiful. Or it would when I finished. I'd already decided I'd give it to Whisper as a gift. She kept telling me to stop buying things for her and Jacob, but she couldn't complain if it was something I'd made with my own two hands. I brought the hammer down again as I shaped the steel. It was my first love, even though I'd also trained with copper and alloys.

Sometimes I made functional things, like bowls or daggers. They were big sellers in the store. Most of the time, I created pieces of art people wanted to display in their homes. The piece for Whisper would be like those. Something she could display in our house, and every time she looked at it, she'd know how much I cared about her.

I snorted. Cared. It didn't even begin to describe my feelings for her. I'd never thought I'd be capable of loving someone. Not in a romantic sense. I loved Jacob, and my brothers, and in my own way I'd loved Whisper even when she'd been a teenager. But the way I loved her now was different. Stronger. And definitely of an intimate nature.

I hadn't said the words, though. I'd come close a

few times. Something had changed this past week, and I knew the time had come. I wanted to finish this piece as quickly as possible. Until it was done, I wouldn't tell Whisper how I felt. Unless she said it first. I wouldn't be a complete dick and not say *I love you* back.

A fist pounded on the door. With a curse, I yelled for whoever it was to come in. I only hoped it wasn't Whisper. When Hawk entered the forge, I breathed a sigh of relief. At least the surprise hadn't been ruined.

"What brings you in here?" I asked.

"I noticed you gave Whisper the ring I'd made. She like it?"

I nodded. "Loves it. Thought it was beautiful, although, she was worried I'd had it made for someone in particular. I had to explain you'd given it to me to hold onto in case I ever had need of a wedding ring."

"Maybe I'm psychic."

I glared at him, and the asshole just laughed.

"Look, I won't lie. I noticed the way you looked at her back before she left. Knew you struggled over it too. I'll admit when I made that ring, I hoped the two of you would find your way back to one another, even though she'd walked out on all of us."

"She did what she felt was right."

"I get it. She had a lot to deal with." He came closer, watching as I hammered the piece of steel. "I asked if she liked it because I made something that would go well with it. Thought you might want to give it to her. You know, when you pull your head out of your ass and realize your wife is pregnant."

The hammer missed the steel and bounced off the anvil on my next swing. I turned to stare at him. "What the fuck?"

"You haven't noticed anything different about Whisper?"

"You've clearly got something to say so fucking say it." Whisper was pregnant? How the hell did he come to that conclusion?

Hawk rubbed a hand over his beard. "As someone who's been through this... or rather, is going through it... have you noticed any changes in her body? Maybe certain parts of her are more sensitive?"

The hammer fell to the floor, and I winced, hoping I hadn't damaged it. Yeah, I'd noticed her breasts seemed more tender, and her nipples were overly sensitive. And then it hit me... she hadn't had a period the entire time we'd been together. Holy shit.

"And the light went on," Hawk said. "Your wife is pregnant, isn't she? Hayley hinted she thought Whisper might be. She didn't know for sure, though. Of course, you know Hayley's hints aren't all that subtle."

"Yeah, I think she is. Why hasn't she said anything?"

"Does she know how you'll react? Did you tell her if you wanted more kids? Could she be scared you'll be upset about it?" Hawk asked.

I wanted to ask Hawk when he'd become such a woman, but I knew Hayley had softened his edges. Or more accurately, nearly losing her had done it. If the Dixie Reapers hadn't put two and two together, then tattled to Beast, my VP might have never known he had a kid on the way, much less found his balls and claimed Hayley.

"She knows I want more kids with her. We talked about having a daughter two months ago. She seemed excited about it."

"Then I don't know, brother. Anyway, give this to her when you're ready." He pulled out a long jewelry box and set it down on a nearby table. "It doesn't match the ring exactly, but it has some of the same design elements. It's also set where I can add some jewels later if you'd like. Maybe one for each kid? Their birthstones or something."

"I'm sure Whisper would love that." I moved over to open the box and check out the necklace. I smiled when I saw it. Yeah, my woman would adore it, especially with the birthstones added in. "Thanks, brother."

"So now that I've gotten that out of the way, I should tell you the other reason I'm here. Hayley saw your art in the shop and really loves the stuff you make. I hoped you might design something she could put on the mantle. I wanted to give it to her for her birthday."

"Consider it done. We'll sit down and discuss a few things once I'm finished with this piece. I'll need to see what you're thinking about and come up with a design. Sound good?"

He nodded. "I'll leave you to it, but seriously... talk to your woman. There's got to be a reason she hasn't said anything. You need to figure out what it is."

I finished my work for the day and headed home. I drove down the main strip and waved to Paris as I passed the coffee shop where she worked. Whisper had helped her get a job as a barista, and the woman had recently moved into her own apartment. The club had helped her with the deposit and some basic essentials to give her a decent start, but Paris had worked her ass off to make something of her life. I had to admit, I was proud of her, and of my wife for thinking of others no matter what shit had landed on her own doorstep.

Gypsy had found a job last week and was now working at a nail salon. Yasmin was the only one who'd been having trouble. She'd been hired, and fired, from two jobs since the night we'd discovered she needed our help. And my wife wouldn't back down. Every time Yasmin came home with bad news, Whisper found more possible jobs for her. I had a feeling it wasn't the places of employment and had more to do with Yasmin's attitude. I'd noticed she didn't seem to like working hard. In fact, I'd be willing to bet she barely did anything at all for any of her previous employers. Which meant we might be stuck with her for a while or would be forced to kick her out.

I didn't think Whisper would take it well if it ended up being option two.

Flossie was still in the fucking wind. Shield had reached out to all the other clubs we called family or friends. None of the hackers had been able to locate her. I didn't know if she'd changed her face, if she was lying dead in a ditch somewhere, or if she'd fled the country. Whatever the case, the woman seemed to be long gone. If she ever came back to town, she wouldn't be breathing for long. Might make me an asshole, but I hoped the bitch was dead. It would serve her right. Poppy and Carina hadn't done anything to Flossie. Their deaths had been senseless. Anyone who killed a child forfeited their life, as far as I was concerned. And I knew the club felt the same way.

The first thing I noticed when I got home were the toys scattered across the front yard. I smiled, thinking about how much my life had changed. There'd been a time I'd have been pulling up to an empty house. Now I had a wife and son inside. Every time I turned around, Brick was buying Jacob something else. Whisper got pissed when I did it, but she couldn't seem to tell her dad to back off. Once I'd figured that much out, I'd decided to accidentally mention to Brick anything I thought Jacob might like or want.

Whisper had caught on quick enough. The first time, she'd read me the riot act about spoiling our son. After the second time, she'd given up. She liked seeing him smile as much as I did. If it had turned him into a rotten kid, then I could have understood. But Jacob remained sweet.

I walked into the house and listened for any clue as to where they might be. It was eerily quiet. I checked each room and didn't see any trace of either of them. By the time I'd reached the bedroom, I'd decided Jacob must not have been home anymore. Since he hadn't been in his room, if he'd heard me, he'd have come running. Whisper lay on her side in the bed, sleeping soundly.

I took a moment to study her. Shadows had started to form under her eyes. I knew she'd been running ragged. Between chasing after Jacob, trying to help the women at the clubhouse, and apparently incubating our baby, she was run off her feet. I slipped off my cut and put it on the dresser before toeing off my boots. I stripped out of the rest of my clothes and went to rinse off in the shower. Sweat had dried to my skin from working in the shop.

I scrubbed myself clean in the shower and toweled off. Not bothering with clothes, I got into bed with my wife, and pulled her into my arms. Smoothing her hair back from her face, I admired how beautiful she was. For that matter, she'd always been pretty. Even as a teenager. Although, I hadn't noticed her as a woman until she'd turned eighteen.

"How did I get so lucky?" I murmured. "You're the best thing to ever happen to me."

She moaned and her eyelashes fluttered as she

slowly opened her eyes. "Victor?"

"You were expecting someone else? I may have to rethink what I just said if you're cheating on me."

She rubbed her face against my chest. "Don't be stupid. Why would I ever want anyone else?"

"Thought maybe you'd wised up and realized I'm not such a great prize. Too damn old, for one."

"Stop!" She leaned up on her elbow and glowered at me. "If you're going to spout that nonsense, you can get the hell out of the bed. You know I don't care about your age. I've been in love with you since I was fifteen."

Her eyes went wide, and she paled. And there it was. She'd said it before I did. So much for waiting until I'd finished her gift. Looked like Hawk had the right idea. I reached over the side of the bed and found my jeans, yanking them closer. I pulled the jewelry box from the pocket and held it out to her. Whisper didn't take it and kept staring at me. I flipped open the lid and finally drew her attention to it.

"Oh, Victor. It's beautiful." She reverently ran her fingers over the necklace.

"Hawk said we could add stones for our children." I touched her chin with my fingertips, making her look at me. "When were you going to tell me?"

"That I love you?" she asked.

"No. I already knew you loved me. I meant about the baby."

She wilted and seemed to withdraw into herself. "You knew?"

"That you love me? Of course. That you're pregnant? No. Not until Hawk pretty much told me I'm a dumbass. I missed the signs. But I want to know why you didn't say anything to me. You knew I wanted more children with you."

"I was waiting," she admitted.

"Why? For the right moment? Were you waiting to see how long before I figured it out?"

"Until you loved me," she said softly. "I wanted to wait until you fell in love with me, the way I've fallen for you. And I know you said you'd never be able to love me. You warned me before you married me."

"Whisper." She looked at me. "Baby, I *do* love you. In fact, I had planned to tell you in a special way, but this changes things. So I'm saying it now. I love you. Adore you. In case you missed it, you and Jacob are the best things to ever happen to me. I don't even want to think about living without either of you."

"You aren't just saying that?"

"No, angel. I'm not. You mean everything to me." I kissed her, taking my time. She clung to me, pressing closer. If I hadn't seen how exhausted she was, I'd have taken things further. Instead, I withdrew. "Knowing we're having another child, that you have a baby growing inside you, is amazing."

"I haven't told Jacob yet either. I'm not sure how he'll react."

"He's going to be excited." I held her closer. "We'll explain how important his role will be as the big brother. I think you'll find he'll be rather eager to meet his baby brother or sister. At least, until the baby gets here and cries all the time."

She playfully smacked me. "Not all babies cry all the time. Jacob was a great baby."

"We'll have to set up a nursery. If you start a wish list online for the furniture and items you want, I bet the club will pitch in. With Lyssa, Hayley, and Danica all pregnant, maybe we could just have one huge party for all of you."

"Sounds fun. I could go for some cake about now."

I chuckled and kissed the top of her head. "I bet you could. I've noticed you have a sweet tooth."

"Wait until we're out somewhere and I'm seven months pregnant. Every time I order dessert, people will stare and whisper about how fat I am. It happened with Jacob. Although, I was ordering fried pies from fast food places since I couldn't afford to eat nicer desserts elsewhere. I did limit myself, though."

"Baby, you eat whatever you want, as long as the doctor says it's okay. Speaking of, we need to set up an appointment for you. I plan to be there for every visit."

"Good. It will be nice to not go through it all alone this time." She curled into me more. "I wish you'd been there with Jacob. When I went into labor, I wanted to call you. I was in so much pain, and I needed you. But I didn't dare reach out. Not after the way I'd left."

"I wish you would have. I'd have been honored to be there with you."

"I've made so many mistakes, Victor, but loving you wasn't one of them."

"I know the feeling, angel. I've done some really bad, fucked up things in my life. Bringing you home with me that day and going after you when I heard about Tommy... those were two things I did right. And just for full disclosure... I probably didn't have to marry you in order for the club to accept you. Being Brick's daughter was enough."

She lifted her head and stared at me. "What does that mean?"

"It means I married you because I wanted to. It was the only way I could think of to make you mine, and make sure you wouldn't leave me again."

"That has to be the sweetest thing I've ever heard." She pressed her lips to mine. "I love you, Victor, and I'm so glad you're mine."

"Me too, baby girl. Me too."

Epilogue

"Victor!" My throat felt raw from screaming his name. I couldn't do this alone. Not again. I refused. "Where. Is. My. Husband!"

"We're looking for him, Mrs. Woods. Please calm down. Your blood pressure is rising and it's not good for the baby."

I growled at her. "You know what else isn't good for the baby? Being born without her daddy here! Find him. Now!"

The woman hurried from the room, and I doubled over as another contraction hit. I felt like I'd landed in the movie *Spaceballs*, when the alien tears its way out of the guy's stomach, then it dances down the counter. Except my alien was my daughter.

I sobbed when the pain started to ebb. I knew he was here. I'd heard his voice in the hallway earlier, but he hadn't made it into the room. Where had he gone and why? If Beast had called him away, I'd tear the man apart as soon as I got out of here. I didn't care if he was the President of the club or not. There were just some moments you didn't ruin with club business, and this was certainly one of them.

When the door opened again, I was ready to yell at whoever it was. Until I saw Forge enter the room. I started crying and couldn't stop as I reached my hand out to him.

"Sorry, angel. I had to take a call from Kye. Clover is running a fever and he panicked."

"Is she okay?"

He nodded. "I think she'll be just fine. He's going to give her some Children's Motrin and keep her hydrated. If the fever doesn't go down, he said he'd take her to the ER."

"I think that's a bit extreme, unless her temp is super high."

Another contraction hit and I screamed as I gripped the rails of the bed. Forge pried my fingers loose and held my hand. He didn't seem to care if I crushed his fingers or not. Good thing too. If he'd bitched, I might have hit him. Or bitten him. Maybe both.

"I've come to a decision," I said as the pain slowed again. "This is it. I hope you're happy with Jacob and Daisy, because we aren't ever having another child. I'm done."

Forge smiled and kissed my brow. "You've given me an incredible son, and I know our daughter will be as perfect as her mother. If you only want two children, that's all we'll have."

"No sex until one of us gets fixed. I don't trust birth control."

"Then I'll get a vasectomy if you're certain you don't want another baby."

I hesitated. "Ask me again in two weeks."

He smiled, then winced as I squeezed his hand when another contraction hit.

"I think it's time. They're coming really close together."

"I'll get the doctor." Forge pried his hand loose from mine.

He stepped into the hall and a minute later, the nurse returned, and the doctor was right on her heels. By the time Daisy made her appearance and vacated my body, I was so tired I could barely keep my eyes open. She fussed and cried as they cleaned her up and checked her out. Then they handed her to me, and all I could do was stare at her. "She's so beautiful," I said. "I think she looks like you."

"No, she's too pretty to look like me. She definitely takes after her mom. I hope she's every bit as sweet as you too."

"Jacob should be here to see her," I said.

"He will be. Brick is bringing him in the morning. We didn't think he'd have the patience to wait at the hospital. This way he gets a good night's sleep, and hopefully so do you."

"I love you, Victor. Thank you for giving me such a perfect little girl, and a happy life. You're my entire world. You and our little family."

"Get some rest, Whisper. I'm not going anywhere, and neither is Daisy. We'll get to know one another while you close your eyes. I'll be sure to wake you when she's ready to eat."

I shook my head. "You can feed her. I won't have any milk. With Jacob, my milk didn't come in for four days. I told the doctor earlier to make sure they had formula for Daisy. Besides, it's not right that only I get to bond with her during feedings."

"Then you sleep as long as you need to. We'll be okay."

I started to close my eyes but fought to stay awake another moment or two. I watched Forge settled into the rocking chair beside my bed with little Daisy in his big, brawny arms. She seemed so tiny as her daddy held her. I reached for my phone and managed to take a picture of the two of them. Forge looked down at the baby in his arms, a tender smile on his face. I knew I'd be framing it and looked forward to taking many more. It only made me sad that I didn't have any of Jacob as a baby with more than just the two of us in it. He deserved to have memories of a father in his life. I'd been making up for lost time and had even started an album full of picture of Jacob and Forge together. And now I'd be starting one for Daisy.

"Close your eyes, Whisper," Forge said, not even looking at me. "I know you're still awake. I can feel you staring."

"Just admiring the view."

"You can do that later. No arguments. Just because I can't spank you right now doesn't mean I can't punish you. I'll just have to be more creative about it."

My cheeks warmed and I smiled as I obeyed and closed my eyes.

I had everything I could ever want. The love and support of friends, my dad was close by, and now my little family was complete. I'd never been happier.

Casper (Naughty Or Nice)
A Bad Boy Romance
Harley Wylde

My marriage is a sham. I've already loved and lost my one and only. Making Carmella Juarez my wife was the only way to save my daughter, but I never intended to stay married. A decade has passed, ten years that I've kept my distance, but now it's time to set things right and free both of us.

I never counted on her being sick and nearly dying. Didn't count on falling for her as I nursed her back to health. But it's the Christmas season and what better time for miracles? My heart isn't as cold and dead as I'd once thought. Carmella has brought me back to life, and now that I've had a taste of the tempting woman who wears my ring, I know that I can't ever let her go.

Chapter One

Carmella

I stared at the enormous rock on my finger and rubbed the golden band with my thumb. I'd always dreamed of getting married, but not once had I ever considered my special day consisting of marrying a man I didn't know, leaving the only home I'd ever had, and being utterly and completely alone. My husband was a powerful man, and feared by many. He was also extremely absent in my life. Casper VanHorne had married me, flown me out of Mexico, then dumped me in some mausoleum of a house only to vanish before I'd even unpacked. It wasn't at all what I'd anticipated. Yes, he was older than me, but I'd looked forward to my marriage. When he'd said he would take care of me, even though love wasn't part of the deal, I'd imagined we would at least live together.

I'd barely been eighteen when he'd married me. At first, I'd thought that's why he had left, and that he'd return before long. Then one year passed, and another. In nearly ten years, I hadn't once seen my husband. It was lonely living here alone. Not to mention, I was twenty-eight and a damn virgin. I was starting to think I would die before ever knowing what it was like to have a man's hands on me, to feel his cock thrusting inside me. My fevered dreams were likely far from what it would really be like if Casper ever came back and claimed me.

As another sharp stabbing pain made my eyes close and my body crumple, I wondered if my husband would return... before it was too late. I'd sworn the staff to secrecy, even the bodyguard Casper had left to watch over me. I'd grown close to the people who ran the house and protected me, even considered them my friends. When I'd first arrived, I hadn't been able to speak any English. Now I was fluent and didn't even use my native tongue anymore.

"Carmella," I heard Bowen shout.

His strong arms wrapped around me, and I felt my body being lifted and carried, likely into the house. The pain had been worse lately, and coming more frequently. I had a feeling I was on borrowed time, but maybe that was for the best. It wasn't that I wanted to die, I really didn't, but I couldn't help but wonder if my husband would be happier if I were gone. I knew he'd been forced into claiming me in order to save his daughter, a daughter he clearly never wanted me to meet.

I'd thought she was younger until he'd explained she was older than me. He didn't look anywhere near old enough to have a fully grown child. There were a few lines around his eyes, but hardly a hint of gray in his hair or beard. At least, last time I'd seen him that was the case. I had no idea what he looked like now.

As the pain eased, my eyes fluttered open and a concerned Bowen was peering down at me.

"He needs to know, Carmella."

"No, he doesn't. He's had no interest in me all this time. The last thing I want is him showing up out of pity. I only wish..." I bit my lip, refusing to say the words.

"I know, sweet girl," Bowen murmured.

We'd grown close over the years, but not in a romantic way. Bowen was more like an older brother than anything else. I gripped his hand as I settled back against my pillows. The frequent headaches that later turned to migraines had started a few years ago, and I'd ignored them at first. After Bowen found me passed out in the sunroom, he'd forced me to go to the doctor.

It had only taken one test to discover the tumor lodged in my brain. The doctor had referred me to a neurosurgeon, who had wanted to start treatment immediately in hopes of avoiding surgery, but I'd refused. They said it appeared to be benign, but the pressure it was putting on my brain was the problem. Thankfully, my husband didn't receive the bills directly. I didn't know how Bowen and Mrs. Weathers had managed to pay for everything without alerting my husband that something was wrong, but they had and I was grateful.

"I can't stand to see you like this," he said. "Please accept the treatment, Carmella. You're young still and have your entire life ahead of you. What you're doing is the same as committing suicide."

"I'm not as strong as I once thought I was," I admitted. "I endured a lot as the illegitimate daughter of the infamous Miguel Juarez. When Casper made me his wife, I'd thought maybe I was going to have a new life. A family of my own, people who would love me. Then he ran and left me here."

Bowen squeezed my hand. "I love you, and so does every other person in this house."

"It's not the same, Bowen. I'm twenty-eight and I've only been on a few dates. The only kiss I ever had was sloppy and gross. I've never… I've never been held by a man who loved me, never experienced passion. Is it wrong for me to want those things?" I asked.

"Of course not, Carmella. Casper would be here if he knew what you were going through. I have no doubt that he'd come and stay with you, take you to the doctor and convince you to start treatment. Don't make me watch you die. They said if you act soon enough, surgery likely won't be needed."

The doctors had said that even though the tumor wasn't cancerous it was still life-threatening. If I had something to live for, then I'd fight with everything I had in me. But what would be the point? I was lonely, so damn lonely. I didn't have a family, and at this rate, I didn't think I ever would. Bowen and Mrs. Weathers were my friends, but they were also paid to stay with me. I knew they cared, but it was different.

I reached up and cupped his whiskery cheek. "I'm sorry, Bowen. I just don't have any fight left in me. There's nothing to fight *for*."

I felt his jaw tighten and watched as his eyes narrowed. I had a feeling I hadn't heard the last from him on the matter. And he wasn't the only one. The cook, Mrs. Weathers, was of the same mind, and so were the two maids and the butler. I knew they'd come to care about me, and I felt the same, but it wasn't enough. I was so damn tired. The pain was debilitating on the best of days, and more and more often, it would make me lose control of the right side of my body, sometimes for an entire day.

I released Bowen and rolled to my side, letting the tears fall silently. He sighed and I heard the door click shut behind him. Left alone with my misery I wondered if maybe I was doing the wrong thing. I had no doubt they were right and Casper would be here if he knew something was wrong, but I wanted him here because he wanted to be, because he cared... not because someone tattled and said I was possibly dying. The last thing I wanted to deal with was his guilty conscience, assuming he even *had* a conscience. I wasn't completely certain what he did, but if he'd had business with my father, I wasn't certain he had a moral compass. It wasn't just that Casper didn't seem to want me. No one had ever wanted me. My mother hadn't, and I'd been an embarrassment to my father who had given me to Casper as a business transaction. What would it be like to be loved? Truly loved?

I drifted for a while, then woke enough to make my way down to the kitchen. I'd missed lunch and my stomach was rumbling and begging for food. Mrs. Weathers had left a lasagna in the oven and fresh rolls in a basket on the counter. We'd finished the Thanksgiving-practice leftovers the day before. Mrs. Weathers had been trying different dishes before the holiday arrived in another two weeks. I fixed a plate and wondered where everyone was hiding. It was unusual for me to not see a single person around the house, especially Bowen.

I'd just taken my last bite of food when a flash of navy blue in the doorway caught my eye. I turned and my fork fell from my fingers, clattering onto the table. My gaze raked over the finest man I'd ever seen, his hair still only had a hint of silver and seemed a bit lighter than I remembered, but there was still power radiating off him. His sweater molded to his biceps, leaving no doubt that the man under the cloth was lethal.

"Carmella," he said, his voice just as smooth as I remembered. "Been a while."

I couldn't speak. It felt like my tongue was stuck to the roof of my mouth as I stared at him. I kept blinking, thinking maybe my poor brain was hallucinating. Wouldn't be the first time I would have seen something no one else could. But if he was here, really here, then...

I stood on shaky legs and walked a little closer, rubbing my hands up and down my leggings. He towered over me and I had to tip my head back to look up at him. Casper's gaze locked on mine, but I couldn't tell what he was thinking. I wished I'd known he was coming. I definitely wouldn't be standing in the kitchen in leggings, a tank top, and a cardigan. It had to be the least sexy thing I owned. My hair was up in a messy bun, and I honestly couldn't remember the last time I'd bothered with makeup or painting my nails. I was a mess.

"You've grown into a beautiful woman," he said. "I'm sure it will be easy for you to find some man to give you the things I couldn't."

Wait. What? The things he *couldn't*? What the hell did that even mean?

"Wh -- what are you talking about?" I asked, my heart nearly stopping.

"I want a divorce, Carmella. Your father is no longer an issue, so I'm going to set us both free from this farce of a marriage."

It felt like the ground was tilting under my feet and I felt my body sway a moment before my knees buckled. I fell to the ground at Casper's feet, tears blurring my vision. I'd waited so long for him to come back, and he finally had... only to say he was getting rid of me? I didn't understand what I'd ever done wrong, what could have possibly made him hate me so much. Or maybe hate was too strong of a word. He'd have to feel something for me to hate me.

It was hard to breathe and I fought not to cry, not in front of him anyway. It was bad enough my legs hadn't held me up. I wouldn't give him the satisfaction of shedding tears, and I wouldn't beg him to stay. I hoped he didn't know he'd broken me with his unfeeling attitude and lack of interest. He didn't kneel to help me up, didn't reach for me at all. I managed to stagger to my feet and pushed past him. My heart ached with the rejection of the man I'd hoped would come to love me one day. He'd said not to expect love from him, but I'd thought... I shook my head. It was a foolish girl's dream and I should have let them go long ago.

I froze at the foot of the stairs, not knowing where to go or what to do. This wasn't my home, not really. It had been my prison for a long time but nothing more. The clothes I had now were all paid for with Casper's money. My purses, the money in my account, everything was his and never mine. My heart hammered in my chest as I turned and walked out the front door, not stopping to look back. I didn't even bother to get my ID, but the first responders and hospital staff all knew me well. If I ended up dead in a ditch, one of them would know to call Bowen.

I made it down the winding driveway and out the front gates without anyone trying to stop me. For the next several hours, I meandered around town, not really having a destination in mind nor feeling the cold. If my father wasn't an issue, as Casper had put it, then he was likely dead. It didn't mean going to Mexico would be safe though. The park across the street looked like a good enough place to sit and figure things out. I found a bench under a tree and eased down onto it, stretching my legs out in front of me.

The air turned even cooler and the sun slowly sank beyond the horizon. As the moon rose high overhead, I realized I was completely alone. No more Bowen. No more Mrs. Weathers. No more maids or butler. I had no one.

The bench creaked and I looked over at my soon to be ex-husband. At least, if he had his way. I didn't understand why he'd bothered to come find me. It wasn't like he actually cared. In all the years we'd been married, it seemed as if he'd never given me a second thought. I didn't believe for one minute that he'd been celibate all this time. He'd never bothered to call me. Oh, he'd talked to Bowen and I guess kept tabs on me, but it wasn't the same as him calling and actually speaking to me, asking me how my day was, or if I needed anything. I'd have gladly told him what I'd needed. Him.

"I wasn't throwing you out of the house," he said.

"It's not my house. I don't belong there. Never did. You've made it clear from the beginning what you thought of me. I'd thought when I grew up a little maybe you'd return, but you never did. Until now."

"It's not personal, Carmella. I married you to save my daughter and to save you as well. I never intended for us to have a real marriage. I've only ever loved one woman, and that's how it will remain until the day I die."

My heart broke a little more at his words. I'd never have that. Never experience a man's love.

"What was it like?" I asked softly.

"What was what like?" he asked.

"Being in love. Loving your wife and having her love you back. What did it feel like?"

He focused on me. "Are you trying to tell me that you've never been in love? Because I have a hard time imagining that, Carmella. Even as an eighteen-year-old, you were beautiful. I'm sure men noticed you everywhere you went."

"No one has ever loved me," I admitted softly. "Not even my parents. If they couldn't love me, why would anyone else?"

I looked up at the moon before standing. Casper didn't stop me as I walked off. I'd never meant to say those things to him, to sound so pathetic. I'd learned to live without love. If the mass in my brain wasn't treated soon, then I wouldn't have to worry about anything for much longer. If it grew much more, the pressure on my brain would end my life. The saddest thing was that no one would even notice I was gone. If Casper was divorcing me, then he'd stop paying Bowen and Mrs. Weathers. The house wasn't mine and neither were they. I had no one.

For the rest of the night, I wandered the small town where Casper had hidden me since our sham of a marriage. Before the sun rose, another spike of pain took me to my knees. The world around me spun, my entire right side going numb. Another burst of pain and everything went dark.

Chapter Two

Casper

I'd followed Carmella for a while, staying in the shadows so she wouldn't see me. I'd thought maybe she would go to a lover's house, or maybe a friend's home. Instead, she'd just walked around town, not really seeming to have any particular direction in mind. When I'd decided she just needed some time to work things out, I'd headed back to the house, thinking she'd return before long. I'd been wrong.

I heard Bowen's steps as he pounded down the stairs about an hour after I'd returned, and I met him in the front entry. His hair was standing upright, and his clothes looked like he'd slept in them. If he'd gone to bed at all, he must have grabbed his dirty clothes and thrown them back on. I'd never seen the man looking anything less than impeccable so I knew something was horribly wrong. His eyes were wide and wild as he looked around the house, as if trying to find something. His gaze landed on the keys near the front door and he snatched them up before rushing outside.

"Bowen, stop," I said, my tone demanding immediate obedience.

He halted but hardly spared me a glance.

"I can't stay, Mr. VanHorne. Carmella needs me."

Carmella? He was on a first name basis with my wife? And was rushing to her side? Maybe she hadn't gone to a lover's home last night because he'd been living under my roof. Anger pushed at me for a moment before I got control of myself. It was ridiculous to feel anything toward a woman I'd never really known. Even if she hadn't been my wife in truth, she'd still carried my name and was mine. I didn't like the thought of someone I'd employed being intimate with her when I'd never had the pleasure.

Bowen didn't move, but I could tell he wanted to leave. I just didn't understand what the hurry was all about. Was Carmella in trouble, or was she just too far from home and needed a ride? No, the look in his eyes said it was something more. Something serious.

"What's going on, Bowen? I paid you to guard her, but I think the two of you grew closer than that. It wasn't very professional of you to fuck the woman under your protection," I said, anger filling me again at the thought of my wife's perfect fucking thighs wrapped around the bodyguard's waist.

Yes, I was dead set against ever falling in love again, but I wasn't fucking blind. The girl I'd married had turned into a stunning woman.

Bowen's eyes went wide a moment and he swallowed hard. "I never touched her, not intimately. I think of Carmella like a sister, Mr. VanHorne, and even if I didn't, I never would have disrespected either of you by making a move on a married woman."

His words cooled my temper a little, but I was still confused why he seemed so panicked.

"Why do you need to rush off? What's going on with my wife?"

Bowen shifted on his feet and the way his eyes darted away from me told me that he was hiding something. The question was how long had he been keeping secrets from me?

"I won't ask again," I said softly.

"She's dying," he blurted, then winced. "Well, possibly might die."

Everything in me went still. "What do you mean she might be dying?"

"Brain tumor. They wanted to treat it or operate, give her a good chance of surviving and having a normal life, but she refused." He looked away, unable to meet my gaze. "She wants to die."

Hearing those words made it feel like someone had shoved a knife through my chest. The sweet, fiery girl I'd married wanted to die? What the fuck had happened to her that she'd want something like that? I'd given her this house, staff to care for her every need, put money into an account for her to shop or have lunch with any friends she made.

"I don't understand," I said. "Why would Carmella want to die?"

The look he gave me would have made a lesser man step back. The fury in his eyes said clearly that he was laying the blame at my feet. Before I could put him in his place, he took me down a few pegs, his every word hitting me like bullets.

"She waited for you," Bowen said. "It broke something inside her when you never returned. Maybe I shouldn't have eavesdropped, but I heard what you said to her. All this time and you finally show up only to tell her that you don't want her? I've never disrespected an employer before, Mr. VanHorne, but you're an asshole. Maybe if I hadn't been so pissed at the way you just tossed her aside, I'd have stuck around long enough to catch her when she left."

Bowen didn't say another word, just turned and headed for the car. He opened the door and paused before getting into it. His gaze locked with mine and he seemed to be struggling with something.

"If you ever gave a shit about what happened to your wife, she's at the hospital. Since I'm her bodyguard, and her husband has never been around, I'm listed as her emergency contact. Someone found her on the sidewalk outside the bakery this morning. She was unresponsive and the doctors…" He shook his head and got into the car, slamming the door.

Carmella was dying? I wasn't sure which was more startling. That my wife had a brain tumor and had chosen to stop living, or the fact that she'd wanted me to come back for her. There was nearly thirty years between us and I'd thought I was doing her a favor by staying away. I'd known if I was anywhere near her, I wouldn't be able to resist those sweet curves of hers. Even at eighteen, she'd been pure temptation for any man, me included.

Before Bowen could pull away from the house, I strode outside and got into the car. He didn't even glance my way, just waited for the car door to shut, then stomped on the gas, sending the car rocketing down the drive and out the gates. A few turns made me wonder if he'd put the car on two wheels, but nothing was slowing him down. He flew into the hospital parking lot and barely took the time to shut off the car before running inside. I followed at a slightly slower pace and saw him frantically gesturing at the front desk.

Stepping up behind him, I caught the eye of the nurse. She gave me the once over, a smile spreading across her lips. The woman leaned forward, the V-neck of her scrubs exposing the edge of a lacy bra. Fucking hell.

"I need information on Carmella VanHorne," I said.

The woman bit her lip and tapped at her keyboard, casting me glances that she probably thought were sexy. I was immune.

"I'm sorry, but Ms. VanHorne is only accepting family," the nurse said.

I gave her the same look I'd given many men, right before I ended their lives. She blanched and glanced at Bowen, as if he might save her.

"For fuck's sake," he said. "Would you just tell the man where his wife is?"

She blinked a few times as if she couldn't process the words. "Wife?"

I pulled out my wallet and flashed her my license. "I'm Casper VanHorne, and my wife, Carmella, was brought in after passing out in front of the bakery. Now, where the fuck is she?"

The woman frantically tapped at her keyboard, then scribbled something on a piece of paper. I took it, and saw she'd written down the room number and the doctor in charge of Carmella's care. I turned to walk off, not bothering to thank her or even see if Bowen was still with me. The elevators weren't far away and I pressed the up button. The damn thing took forever to reach the fifth floor but I easily found Carmella's room. She looked so damn still lying in the bed, her eyes closed.

Her red hair was fanned across the pillow and I stared at it. When I'd married her, it had been a dark brown. I had to admit, I liked the red. I didn't know when or why she'd colored it, but it didn't matter. It seemed I'd fucked up by leaving her alone for so long. I'd thought it was the right thing to do. I needed her to wake up so we could have a little chat about her throwing her life away. Just because I was incapable of loving someone again, it didn't mean she was unlovable or that no one would ever love her.

I sat on the edge of her bed and took her hand. It looked so small in mine. My memory flashed back to our wedding day. She'd worn a pretty white dress with blue embroidery, her hair down and shining in a cascade of curls. I'd kept reminding myself she was just a kid, but she'd been breathtaking. It was part of why I'd left her here alone. I'd had my one true love and my heart was no longer mine to give. Someone like Carmella deserved more than I could offer.

"Mr. VanHorne?" a voice asked from behind me.

I turned and assessed the man standing in the doorway. His badge said he was Dr. Peterson. He looked at me, expectantly, and I realized he was waiting for me to confirm my identity. There were bonuses to having a little work done here and there, lightening my hair and beard. It kept my enemies on their toes a little since they were expecting an old man. Instead of fifty-seven, I looked closer to my mid-forties. My face hadn't really changed over the years. I might have some lines removed, and I'd admittedly had my nose altered a little five years ago, but for the most part I hated going under the knife if it wasn't necessary. Plastic surgery was at least a once every five to ten years solution. Disguises had to be worn daily and were a pain in the fucking ass. If I wanted to keep my daughter and grandkids safe, then it was better that I change my appearance every so often.

"That's me," I said.

"Your wife's condition has worsened. I've asked Mrs. VanHorne multiple times to accept treatment for her tumor, but she's refused. I'm afraid it's reached the point where we need to remove the mass. From the tests we've run, it's non-cancerous, but it's putting a lot of pressure on her brain as it grows."

"As her husband, can I sign whatever is required for her to have the surgery?" I asked.

He hesitated, his gaze going to Carmella. "She's expressed her desire to let the tumor run its course."

"And if she were your wife?" I asked.

He smiled faintly. "Husband, but I get the point. And yes, I would sign the papers and have the operation done before he had a chance to say no. I'll have a nurse bring the forms to you and I'll have the OR prepped."

"What can I expect on the backside of this?" I asked. "Personality changes? Will she lose motor function?"

"If we're able to get all the mass, then she should heal in about four to eight weeks. Right now, the mass is causing her to lose feeling and function in the right side of her body. It's not constant, which is unusual. I can't say for certain how she'll react to having the tumor out, but I believe it will be a favorable outcome."

I nodded and turned back to Carmella. "Get me the papers."

I held my wife's hand and wished I could take back the last decade. I should have never stuffed her in that house and left her. She'd been vulnerable. A young, scared woman and I'd just abandoned her. What kind of monster did that make me? I might kill people for a living, but I'd always prided myself on protecting women and children. I'd failed my wife, and I refused to fail her again.

The nurse came in with the papers. I signed everything, then held Carmella's hand until they came to take her to surgery. Bowen was in the waiting area and I sat next to him. Part of me was furious he hadn't said something sooner, but at the same time, he'd remained loyal to Carmella. I couldn't fault him for that.

"Surgery will take three to five hours, as long as everything goes according to plan," I said.

He gave me a startled look. "She's having the surgery?"

"Didn't give her a choice. She was still passed out, so I signed the consent forms to have it done. I'm sure she'll be pissed when she wakes up, but at least she'll be alive."

Bowen breathed out hard and I noticed the tension ease from his body. I still wasn't convinced he didn't think of Carmella as something more than a friend or younger sibling, but I couldn't deny that he cared about her. Even if I didn't like how close they'd become, I was also glad she'd had a shoulder to cry on when she'd needed one. It made my chest ache that I might have been the cause of those tears. Instead of giving her freedom, I'd made her a prisoner in her own home, made her feel unworthy of being loved. I really needed to kick my own ass when all this was over.

"Why didn't you ever come back?" Bowen asked. "Or call and talk to her?"

"I was trying to give her space. I figured she'd find someone closer to her age who would interest her. It never crossed my mind she'd stay faithful, or actually want me around."

Bowen snorted and didn't say anything. Probably for the best. If he'd called me on being a dumbass, I might have been compelled to hurt him. I didn't think Carmella would appreciate that very much. She was going to be mad enough I'd forced the surgery on her when she wasn't able to say no.

The time passed slowly. When the doctor came to inform me that the surgery had been a success, the mass had been fully removed, and Carmella was in recovery, it felt like I could breathe easier. I hadn't realized until that moment exactly how upset I was over the situation. Yeah, I'd been mad at myself for not being here and realizing things were bad, but the idea she wouldn't make it through the surgery hadn't really been front and center in my thoughts. Or I hadn't thought it was.

Bowen left, leaving me alone. I hoped I'd have some time with Carmella. Although, I had to wonder if it was more because he knew she'd be pissed when she realized what I'd done. I decided to see about waiting with her in recovery, wanting to be there when she woke up. At first, the nurse refused to let me go back, but after a bit of cajoling she let me through. I pulled up a chair next to Carmella's bed and reached for her hand. I didn't know how long it would take for her to wake up, but I'd be here no matter if I had to sit in the hard-ass chair for hours.

When her eyes slowly fluttered open and she groaned, I gave her hand a slight squeeze. Her gaze flitted over to mine and her lips parted.

"Welcome back," I said.

"Did I pass out again?" She frowned and tried to reach for her head, but I pulled her hand away from the bandages. "What happened?"

"Your doctor discussed your options with me. I signed off on the surgery. They removed the tumor."

There was a flash of surprise in her eyes, quickly followed by anger, frustration, then curiosity. She glanced down at her hand in mine, but she didn't pull away. There was a cautious hope when her gaze lifted to mine again.

"Why are you here?" she asked. "You wanted a divorce."

"I'm not going anywhere, Carmella. You'll need some help until you're back on your feet. The doc said it could take four to eight weeks before you're recovered."

"Right. *Then* you'll leave." She looked away. "Just go now. If you want me to stay at the house, fine.

Bowen and Mrs. Weathers can help me just like they have all this time. I don't need you, Casper."

I was good at reading people. Always had been. And right now, I could tell that my wife was lying through her damn teeth. She did need me, but she didn't *want* to need me. Sure, Bowen and Mrs. Weathers had taken good care of her over the years, but right now she needed her husband.

"If I leave, you're going with me," I said.

She gave a slight gasp. "What?"

"Did you think that was the only house I own?" I asked, my eyebrow arched. "I bought a place not too far from my daughter. We can go there while you recuperate. The warmer southern climate might be better for you."

She pulled her hand from mine and looked away. "You didn't want me to meet your family. Remember?"

She wasn't exactly wrong. I hadn't wanted her to meet them. I didn't need my daughter thinking that I'd replaced her mother, or for my grandkids to get confused. Carmella wouldn't be their grandmother. Once she was better, we'd part ways. I'd make sure she had enough to get a new start somewhere, and I'd have my jet take her anywhere in the world she wanted.

I hadn't really planned for her to meet Isabella and the kids. Yes, my Alabama home was near the Dixie Reapers, but not in the same town. It was close enough for a visit but far enough that Carmella could stay there, and my family would never know. *Now you're being an asshole.*

I sighed and tipped my head back, pinching the bridge of my nose. This is why I'd avoided remarrying. Well, that and my one and only love had died. No way I'd ever experience that again. That kind of love only happened once in a lifetime. I'd been lucky to find it the first time. Having it again? Never happen, especially not to a guy like me.

"You're coming with me, Carmella. I'm not asking. You need help right now."

"I don't know why you suddenly care. You haven't from the beginning. I was just a way to save your precious Isabella, not even good enough to meet her or your grandchildren. I'm your dirty little secret, locked away where no one can find out. You should have just let the tumor kill me."

I growled and stood so fast the chair fell over. Pointing a finger at her, I tried damn hard not to bare my teeth like a feral beast.

"Stop that shit right now! I told you from the beginning I'd only ever love one woman. You married me anyway."

"I needed to escape my father and Mexico. Do you think I'd have married a heartless, soulless man if given a choice?" she shot back.

Her barb made a direct hit and I staggered back a step, then turned and walked out. I hadn't cleared the doorway before I heard her crying. It made my chest hurt again and I rubbed the area. Whether she liked it or not, I wasn't going to leave her in the care of her bodyguard. She was going home with me, and that was final.

Chapter Three

Carmella

The rain was pinging off the windows and the trees swayed with the gusts from the incoming storm. Casper had made sure the generator was ready in case we lost power, and he'd stacked logs by the fireplace with more in the garage. I'd lost the battle and the hospital had released me into his care, even made him sign paperwork. They'd all conspired against me. My fingers curled until my nails pressed into my palms. The worst part was how sweet he'd been to me the last three weeks.

I'd been to a local neurologist this morning and gotten the all clear. Even though they'd estimated four weeks of recovery, the doctor had said I could resume most normal activities, including sex. Since Casper had been in the room with me, I'd blushed like the virgin I am and ignored both men. I didn't have clearance to do anything crazy like go to an amusement park and ride the thrill rides, but it seemed I'd healed quickly with no side effects. Although, I'd been warned that some side effects wouldn't show for a few weeks or months, so I wasn't one hundred percent free and clear just yet.

"I gave Mrs. Chambers the night off," Casper said as he came into the room and sat on the chair across from me. I ignored him and kept watching the rain. Petty, yes. Childish, yes. But I didn't care.

Casper sighed and looked around the room before returning his gaze to me. I could see him from the corner of my eye, but I hoped he didn't know I was trying to discreetly observe him.

"Look, Carmella. You can't stay pissed at me forever. I asked Mrs. Chambers to make enchiladas and tacos for dinner. She even used your rice recipe."

I snorted. I loved Mrs. Chambers. She was a sweet old woman, but she couldn't make food spicy enough to suit me. She did try though, so there was that. At least we'd have food to eat if the storm was as bad as they were saying. I'd noticed that Casper had also stocked canned goods, rice, noodles, and a ton of water in crates in a side room off the garage. I'd asked him about it, and he'd said he liked being prepared. He also had a lot of gas for the generator, but I didn't know if it would be enough to keep the essentials going for more than a day or two.

"You can't hate me forever," he said. "I did what was necessary to keep you alive, Carmella."

"No one asked you to."

"You are so fucking stubborn!" He slammed his hands down on the arms of the chair, then stood. "Fine. You don't want me here, I'll leave you alone. I'll go stay in the fucking guest house."

As he stormed from the room, I couldn't hold back my tears. Did I want him to leave? Not really, but he couldn't give me the one thing I *did* want from him. He'd spent our marriage regretting that he'd been forced to marry me. I'd spent that time wishing he'd come home, start a life with me, show me what it was like to be a wife in truth. I'd been so stupid, so naïve. The world didn't work that way. Men like Casper didn't fall for pathetic women like me.

I stood and made my way through the house. If Casper was going to sleep elsewhere, then there was no point in leaving all the lights on. I could wallow in my bed just as well as downstairs. Flipping the switches one room at a time, my hand froze as I reached for the one in the kitchen. I could have sworn I saw a shadow move past the window. The lights went out. No, not the lights. Everything had gone off. I waited, knowing the generator was prepped and ready, but it never started up.

My heart thundered in my chest as I took a cautious step back and another. I didn't know why Casper would be around the side of the house, lurking outside the kitchen. There was a faint click, like a lock turning, and then the door off the kitchen opened. A figure in all black crept inside, a gun clutched in his hand, and I knew I was in serious trouble.

Trying to move slowly enough I wouldn't be noticed, I inched farther back into the shadows of the room behind me. I'd just stepped into total darkness when a hand pressed to my mouth and I went stiff. Then the scent that teased my nose set me at ease. *Casper.*

"Stay quiet and stay close," he whispered in my ear.

I nodded that I understood, and he released me. I put my fingers through his belt loop and stayed as close as I could. We made our way through the lower level of the house and up the stairs. When we reached the master bedroom, he opened the closet, popped open a panel and entered a code. A hidden door released, and Casper shoved me inside.

"Stay there and don't come out. I'll come back for you when it's safe."

"What if you don't come back?" I asked, my fear growing and clawing at the inside my belly like a living, breathing monster.

He hesitated only a moment. "Passcode is the month, day, and year of your birthday followed by the month and day of our wedding."

I blinked in surprise. He'd used our marriage and my birthday for his code? Why? It was obvious I'd never meant anything to him. Had I been wrong about him forgetting me completely? I nodded, then he locked me into the small space.

There was a bank of black-and-white monitors on the wall. The screens were the only source of light, and I watched in horror as three men searched the house. Were they looking for Casper? I couldn't think of any other reason for them to be there, unless they just wanted to rob the place. That didn't seem likely as they passed by valuable knickknacks and paintings. Another shadow slunk along the perimeter of the living room and I gasped as Casper snuck up behind one of the intruders and snapped his neck.

My eyes were wide as he went room by room, taking them down. The last one wasn't as easy. I couldn't hear anything, so I didn't know if maybe he'd caught on. Casper managed to disarm the man and threw a punch. The guy only smiled, and it looked like blood covered his teeth. He spat on the floor and went after Casper. They grappled and fought, landing blow after blow. I started to worry that maybe my husband had met his match when he moved so fast that I couldn't even tell what he'd done. I only knew one minute the two men were fighting and the next the intruder was dead on the floor. Or I assumed he was dead.

Casper dragged the bodies from the house, and then I saw him moving toward the master bedroom. When the panic room door opened, I flung myself into his arms. I didn't care that I'd been upset with him, or that he didn't want me. He was alive and that was all that mattered.

He held me tight, stroking his hand down my hair. "Easy. They're gone. You're safe, Carmella."

"Who were those men? What did they want?"

He shook his head. "I'm not sure, but I intend to

find out. Right now, I need to get you out of here. Until I know it's safe, I don't want you in the house."

I pulled back and looked up at him. "But where will I go?"

Casper only hesitated a moment. "Dixie Reapers' compound."

My jaw dropped a little. He wanted me to go to… the Dixie Reapers? That's where his daughter lived, and his grandkids. He'd said he didn't want us to meet. Why would he send me there? He had to be kidding, right?

"Casper, why would you send me there?"

"Because I know they'll keep you safe."

I shook my head. No. He'd made it clear he didn't want me near his family. I wasn't going to stay with them just because some men had broken into the house. My father hadn't exactly kept me safe over the years. I wasn't a stranger to men coming after me, wanting me to die. I wouldn't run and hide like a good little girl.

"No."

He scowled. "What the fuck do you mean 'no'?"

"I'm not running away. There's no reason I can't stay here. They cut the power to the house. You just need to set it up so the generator kicks on automatically when that happens. Then no one can take us by surprise again."

"Carmella, I don't think you understand."

I pulled away from him completely and put some space between us. I didn't understand? Like it was difficult? Did my poor little woman's brain just not comprehend that men had broken into the house?

"Are you kidding me right now?" I crossed my arms and pressed my lips together. "Do you remember who my father is? Do you think I'm a stranger to the dangers of being with a man like you? I know you don't obey the law, Casper. If you did, you never would have made a deal with my... sperm donor."

He growled and ran a hand through his hair. "Jesus fucking Christ."

"I knew when I married you that there might be times I wasn't safe, that I was signing on for a lifetime of keeping up my guard. I made a mistake and relaxed, since nothing has happened since we married, but it won't happen again."

Casper walked off, slamming the bedroom door behind him. I stared at it a moment not quite certain what to do. Was I supposed to just wait here? It wasn't even my room. He hadn't exactly said I needed to stay put. I decided to go wait in my own room. Being in Casper's felt... like I was intruding on his privacy or something. We were married in name only. I didn't have a right to be in here.

I walked silently down the hall to the guest room, pushed the door open, and stepped inside. I closed it and twisted the lock. If Casper worried someone might still be around, then that little lock made me feel somewhat safer. I had no doubt a man could bust through the door, but it might take them a minute or two and give me time to come up with a hiding place or escape route.

Even though it wasn't incredibly late, I found that I was more tired than usual. Probably the excitement of having to hide in the panic room. Kicking off my shoes, I curled up on the bed and closed my eyes. At one time, I'd thought if Casper came for me that things would change. I'd have a family, be happy. I placed a hand over my belly and wondered if I'd ever have children. For that matter, would I ever even have sex?

There were times I wondered if I wouldn't have been better off staying in Mexico. My father had demanded that I leave, that Casper marry me and take me away, but I could have stayed and hidden in a small rural village. Maybe if I'd done that, if I'd faked a marriage to Casper, then I'd have had a life. I'd only traded one prison for another.

There was a knock on the door. "Carmella, come out so we can talk."

I snorted and buried my face in my pillow. Why would I want to talk to him? All he'd do was tell me what he thought I wanted to hear, or go on and on about how things would never work between us. I didn't need him to say it another hundred times. I got it. He didn't want me. It wasn't like I hadn't heard that before, from my own father, no less.

"There's nothing to discuss. I'll stay here until you're ready to sign the divorce papers. No point in stressing out your family."

There was a *thunk* like he'd dropped his head to the door, or maybe hit it with his fist. Hard to say for certain.

"Carmella, honey… Please don't do this."

Do what? Try and be logical about it? I wouldn't beg him to let me stay, to remain married to me. I did have at least a little pride left.

"Just go away, Casper. We don't have to talk, or share meals, or spend time together at all. You do whatever you need to, and I'll just… read or something."

He gave a humorless laugh.

"Casper, really. It's fine. You want a divorce, then I'll sign whatever you give me. You don't have to pretend like you suddenly care. You never have." The words hurt to say, but they were true. My plan to just let the tumor decide my fate hadn't worked out. Casper had seen to that. Now that it looked like I would be alive for a while, I needed to figure things out. Where would I go? What would I do?

Some people might be excited over a chance to start over. That was the last thing I wanted. It was hard to "start over" when you'd never really begun your life. I'd been my father's daughter in Mexico, a puppet. Then I'd become Casper's wife, but had been more like a ghost haunting the house he'd stuffed me in. I didn't know who I was, or who I wanted to be. I just knew that I wanted to be loved. Was that really so unreasonable?

I gave a startled yelp when the door swung open. Casper put away the tools he'd used to pick the lock, then strolled inside. He didn't stop until he reached the bed, then he folded his arms and stared down at me. Why did he have to look sexy even doing that? I'd always found my husband attractive, which just made everything even worse.

"What makes you think I don't give a shit what happens to you?" he asked. "I shoved you in that panic room to keep you alive."

"Only because you felt guilty."

He ran a hand down his face and huffed. "Guilty. That's a good one, sweetheart. I've never felt guilty about a damn thing, except you. I hated that I'd made you feel so unwanted, so unloved that you were going to die. I hated that I'd avoided you for all these years instead of checking on you in person, or at least speaking to you. Maybe then I'd have known something was wrong."

"You don't need to say all that. I just misunderstood when we got married. I'd thought you wanted some time and would return. You'd never said as much so it's on me for assuming that's what you meant."

He rolled his neck and it cracked a few times, then he settled on the edge of the bed. Casper reached for my hand and twined his fingers with mine. I stared at our clasped hands, a weird flutter in my chest and stomach. I thought about pulling away, but I honestly enjoyed his touch a little too much.

"I'm going to call Torch and see if we can stay at the Reapers' compound," he said. "We won't stay with him and Isabella, but I'd feel better if you were behind their gates. I'm sure there's a spot we can hunker down while I figure out why those men were here."

"If we're there, then you know your daughter will come by. I don't want things to be more difficult than they already are."

He lifted my hand and kissed the back of it, making my breath catch. He'd never done anything like that before. My gaze met and held his, trying to determine what he was thinking or feeling. But as usual, Casper was a blank slate.

"Will it really bother you to be there?" he asked.

I nodded. The last thing I wanted was to meet his family, get attached, then never see them again. I knew he had grandchildren and I'd always loved kids. I'd hoped to have a few myself one day.

"Then we'll go to my cabin."

"Cabin?" I asked.

"In the Smoky Mountains. You'll like it there. Nice and quiet, and we'll probably get some snow. Have you ever seen snow?"

"Not in person."

He nodded. "Then that's where we'll go. No one knows about it but my family so it should be safe. I'll figure out who broke in to the house here and decide what we'll do next."

"Guess that means I need to pack."

"Pack whatever you want, but we can buy more when we get there. Anything you own won't be near warm enough when the snow hits."

He hesitated a second, kissed my cheek, then stood and walked out. I lifted a hand to press to the spot where his lips had met my skin, baffled at what the hell was going on. It was almost like I was dealing with two different Caspers. One was the gruff asshole who'd demanded a divorce without a shred of compassion. The other was... Well, the other seemed like the kind of man I'd want to hold onto, one I'd want to stay married to, but I didn't think that would happen. Whatever was causing this change in Casper, I doubted it would last. Once the danger had passed, he'd want me gone again.

I just hoped I didn't fall in love with him before that. My poor heart couldn't handle it.

Chapter Four

Casper

I was fucked. Well and truly fucked, and not in the good way. When I'd noticed someone breaking into the house, my first thought had been Carmella. Seeing one of those assholes so close to her had sent me into a rage. As I'd taken them out one by one, I'd tried not to worry why it mattered so much. She was my wife and I was honor-bound to protect her. That's it. I'd tried to tell myself that anyway. In my gut, I knew better. She mattered more to me than she should.

Hearing her say that she'd rather stay here, in danger, than go meet my daughter and grandkids... it made me realize I'd been the biggest asshole on the fucking planet. Carmella was a sweetheart and I'd just trampled right over her. Seeing the defeated look in her eyes, the acceptance that I didn't want her, it had about killed me. It felt like someone was reaching into my chest and squeezing my heart. She might as well have ripped it out and stomped it to dust.

I'd thought I was beyond caring about anyone other than Isabella or my grandkids. It seemed I was wrong.

I'd called the airstrip and my jet was being fueled. My bag was packed, but I had more shit at the cabin. I'd also done a bit of shopping online and arranged for some things to be delivered to the cabin. Christmas was fast approaching, and I had every intention of spending it there with Carmella. She just didn't know it yet. I'd always sent a little trinket to her each holiday and for her birthday, but I knew now it had been a meaningless gesture. She'd have much preferred an actual visit with no gifts. This year would be different. I'd make sure of it.

While she packed and did whatever the fuck women did to prepare for a trip, I rummaged through the pockets of the men who had dared to come after me. There wasn't much to find except a phone on one of them. It was just a basic flip phone with one text showing. Not even something that seemed to pertain to them breaking into my house. I used my phone to snap a picture. After I made arrangements with a clean-up crew, I carried the flip phone inside, dropped it into a padded mailer, then made another call.

"Need a pickup," I said the nameless person on the other end.

"Leave it in the usual place."

"It will be there in two minutes and needs to go directly to Wire at the Dixie Reapers. No one else touches it."

I got a grunt for a response and nothing else, but I knew they would follow my instructions.

Ending the call, I carried the package out back and hid it amongst the woodpile on the back porch. While this house wasn't as safe as my cabin, I'd hoped that Carmella wouldn't be in danger here. It seemed I'd been wrong. I hoped the package was delivered soon and Wire would be able to pull something from the device once it reached him. I had an idea who sent the men, but I wanted to be sure before I plotted my revenge. It was one thing to come after me when I was alone, but those fuckers had put my wife in danger, and that I wouldn't tolerate.

Probably my own fucking fault. I'd kept Carmella a secret. Torch and Isabella knew of her, but other than a mention here and there, I'd tried to keep conversations away from the subject of my wife. I'd done it to protect her, even though she thought I was keeping her from my family. Maybe it had started that way, but once I'd seen how sweet she was, realized that her sexy curves made me want to break my promise, I'd known that I needed to keep her as far from my life as possible.

I'd done too good a job of it until now. There was just one problem. I wasn't sure that I could still let her go when the time came. The thought of having someone to come home to, a woman who was beautiful and sweet, was incredibly tempting. I'd had my share of mistresses over the years, but no one I couldn't leave without a single regret. With Carmella, I had no doubt that I'd regret letting her go. She was mine, even if I hadn't claimed her.

She carried a bag into the living room and set it down. Her lower lip looked bruised and I knew she'd either been biting it or chewing on it. The fact she was nervous bothered me. I'd never hurt her, not intentionally anyway. I'd done enough damage just by being absent.

"Jet should be ready by the time we reach the airstrip."

Carmella nodded and reached for her bag again, but I stopped her. No fucking way was I going to let my wife carry her own damn bag. I picked it up, then led the way out to the car. Stowing our bags in the back seat, I stared at them a moment and tried to analyze the strange feeling in my chest. Seeing Carmella's red luggage next to mine didn't exactly send me running for the hills. With any other woman, I'd have felt like I was choking when things got too domesticated. Not the case with Carmella.

Everything had seemed so clear-cut when I'd gone to ask for a divorce, or rather to inform her we were getting one. Watching over her in the hospital and later at one of my many homes had changed things. Finding out she'd had no one all these years except the bodyguard and staff I'd hired made me feel lower than low. I'd always prided myself on treating women decently. Even the ones I fucked and discarded knew the score going in. But Carmella hadn't been given a choice. She'd been a pawn and nothing more. I'd only been thinking of keeping my family safe, and her father had wanted her gone.

We got in the car and I drove to the airstrip, keeping an eye out for more trouble. Not knowing who those men were or what they wanted had me on edge. There was no telling when or where another attack would come from. I hoped that Wire could pull something off the phone soon. If I didn't have Carmella with me, things would be different. Having her right in the path of danger changed everything.

The jet was ready when we arrived. My wife hadn't said a damn word the entire car ride to the airstrip, and I wondered if I'd get the silent treatment all the way to East Tennessee. Thankfully, it wasn't a very long flight, and there was plenty I could do. While I'd made some changes to my life the last few years, my hands weren't completely clean. I doubted they ever would be. I'd made enough money I never had to work again, but sitting idle would drive me crazy. The only way I'd completely retire is if I died. Or found another way to occupy my time.

Our bags were loaded and I helped Carmella up the steps. I urged her into a seat by the window, hoping she'd enjoy the view. I didn't know if she'd flown any time other than when I'd brought her here from Mexico. The trip from the hospital had been by car since she hadn't been healed enough for air travel.

I took the seat next to her and pulled out some files from a briefcase I kept with me. There were a few threats I'd received in the last several weeks and I hadn't taken them seriously. Now I was wondering if I'd overlooked something. In general, the men coming for me weren't anything to be concerned about, but if they had help... I knew there were plenty of men and organizations around the globe who would love to see me taken down. Maybe one day they would succeed, but I hoped that Carmella would stay safe if that ever happened.

"Why do you have a file on Raul Montenegro?" Carmella asked.

I slowly turned to look at her. "How do you know Montenegro?"

She had her gaze locked on the file, but I noticed she'd turned pale. There was fear lurking in her eyes, and it made me want to reach out and crush Montenegro. I had no idea what he'd done to her, but he'd be punished for it.

"Carmella." My voice had just enough bite she jerked her gaze to mine. "What did he do to you?"

Her lower lip trembled. "My father invited him to Mexico when I was fifteen. I'd never been allowed into his home. His dirty little secret. When I received his summons, I was so excited. I thought maybe he would finally love me."

I reached out to cup her cheek. She leaned into my touch, her eyes sliding shut, as she took a shuddering breath.

"My father only wanted me there because Montenegro liked young girls."

A growl rose in my throat before I could hold it back. That bastard! If he'd touched her, I'd fucking kill him!

"Montenegro made it seem as if he were interested. I hated the way he looked at me, the coldness in his eyes. He asked my father if he could strip and fuck me right then and there. My father gave his blessing, and I promptly threw up."

I tried not to react, tried to keep my rage in check.

"Montenegro backhanded me for messing up his shoes, then demanded my father bring him someone younger. I was banished from the house and never permitted to return, for which I was grateful, but I knew one day my father would find a way to make me pay for humiliating him."

And now I was receiving threats from Montenegro. I didn't think it was a coincidence. I just wasn't certain why he'd come for me now, or her. If he preferred little girls -- sick fuck! -- then why would he be interested in a fully grown Carmella? She was close to thirty now.

"Why do you have a file for him?" Carmella asked again. "Casper, you can't... you can't do business with him. He's dangerous, mean, and he has no soul."

"Honey, I'm not doing business with him. He's behind some threats I've received lately. I didn't understand why, but now I think I do. He knows I have you, but I don't understand why he'd want you now."

"Because I'm all grown up?" she asked.

I nodded.

"It was so long ago, Casper. Maybe the two things aren't related. I can't imagine that someone like him would want an adult woman. Why now? Why wait so long? Wouldn't it have been better to come take me while we weren't together? He has to know that snatching me while I'm under your direct protection would be suicidal."

I smirked a little. "What do you know about it?"

She blinked twice, then gave a delicate snort. "Casper, I'm not stupid. The fact my father gave me to you was enough of a clue. You're a badass, maybe not part of a cartel, but I know you're a powerful man. The kind who shouldn't be trifled with."

I stroked my finger down her nose. "Such a smart girl. Beautiful too."

I wasn't going to tell her exactly what I'd done to earn my money. Better that she didn't know. I hadn't exactly kept it from her, but then we hadn't spent a lot of time together. She seemed to know I was a dangerous man, and she wasn't wrong. I just didn't want to confess that I killed people for a living. After our marriage, I'd made arrangements to fly back to the US, gotten her settled in her new home, and I'd left again. Then I did the cowardly thing and stayed gone for a decade. Right now, I was kicking my own ass over that one.

I pulled my phone from my pocket and shot off a message to Wire, then shut off the device. Once we'd landed, I'd see if he'd found anything yet. Until then, I'd put all this shit away and spend time with my wife. Something I should have done years ago. Maybe it wasn't too late to get to know her. The woman she'd grown to be was intriguing, and really damn tempting.

The jet jolted as it moved forward and soon we were lifting into the air.

I put the files away, and reached for Carmella's hand, twining our fingers together.

"What are you doing?" she asked.

"I'm hoping my wife will give me a chance to get to know her. We have over two hours before we land."

She looked up at me, her eyes full of hope and a little bit of fear. Poor girl. I owed her so damn much.

Not material things, but… my time. Patience. And so much more.

"You want to get to know me?" she asked, her voice a near whisper.

"Yeah. I do." I looked down at our clasped hands. "I think I owe it to the both of us to find out about the remarkable woman I married."

"She's not all that special."

I leaned closer and brushed my lips over her cheek. Her indrawn breath and the way she tensed said perhaps it was too much too soon. Then her gaze lifted and held mine. Before I knew what she was doing, Carmella had pressed her lips to mine. Not giving her a chance to pull away or change her mind, I grasped a handful of her hair and held her in place as my lips moved over hers. I flicked my tongue across her lower lip, groaning at the sweet taste of her.

Carmella opened and let me in, and I was fucking gone. Deepening the kiss, I knew then and there why I'd never kissed her before. Not really, truly kissed her. Because now that I had, I knew I didn't want to ever kiss another woman for as long as I lived. Carmella was mine, and I was never letting her go. Divorce? Not happening. Even if she decided she wanted one, I'd just tie her down and convince her otherwise.

Unfastening her seat belt, I hauled her out of her seat and onto my lap. She gave a slight squeak and gripped my shoulders, her ass pressing against my cock. I'd never been harder in my life than I was right now. Never been tempted more either. She was all soft and curvy, a perfect fit as I held her close. I'd loved my first wife, the mother of my only child, but we'd had a different kind of connection -- a friendship that had grown into more. With Isabella's mother, it had felt more like a slow simmer. But Carmella? She made me feel like I had fire in my veins.

I kissed her like it would be our last. Now there wasn't an armrest between us, I decided to explore. While my lips devoured hers, I slid my hand from her hip, up her soft stomach, and I cupped her breast. Carmella moaned into my mouth, her nipple hardening against my fingers as I lightly stroked it. That one touch was enough to make her melt into me. I worked my hand under her sweater, then tugged at her lacy bra. Her breast popped free and I wished like hell I could see her.

A quick pinch of her nipple made her cry out and go tight. The shocked gasp she gave made me wonder what kind of lovers she'd had that they hadn't ensured she'd been properly pleasured. Then the thought of other men touching her made me want to go kill them all. I pulled away only long enough to strip her sweater off.

Carmella's gaze shot around the small cabin of the jet, but I knew we were alone except the pilot and co-pilot. Neither would be leaving the cockpit if they knew what was good for them. The scrap of lace looked sexy as hell, but it needed to go. I popped the clasp on her bra and removed it, dropping it on the floor with her top. Bared to my view, she tried to cover herself, but I pried her hands away from her breasts.

"You're stunning. Don't hide from me."

A flush rose to her cheeks as she let me look my fill. I cupped one of the plump mounds, then wrapped my lips around her nipple. I flicked my tongue against the bud before giving it a slight bite.

"Casper!"

While I licked and tasted her breasts, I reached down to pull off her shoes and started working her leggings down her thighs. She squirmed and begged, the scent of her arousal filling the cabin of the jet. One touch to the material covering her pussy and I felt how soaked she was, how much she wanted me. Some caveman part of my brain made me want to beat my chest, toss her over my shoulder, and drag her off to fuck her for hours. Shoving the material aside, I stroked her wet lips before shoving a finger inside her tight sheath. *Fuck!* So perfect! My dick ached at the thought of being inside her.

I pushed my finger in and out, and worked her clit with my thumb. Carmella parted her thighs more, lifting her ass. My lips tugged on her nipple again, and she came. The gush of her release and the sweet cries she made were enough to make me unfasten my seat belt and stand with her in my arms. I carried her over to the couch, jerked off her panties, and started unfastening my pants.

My heart hammered in my chest as I positioned her the way I wanted, bent over the back, her ass in the air. I pushed her thighs apart, groaning at the sight of her slick, swollen pussy. She was fucking perfection, and she was mine!

I shoved my pants down my thighs and gripped her hips. Lining up with her entrance, I sank deep with one hard thrust. It felt like Carmella locked into place, not even breathing. And that's when I realized something... My sweet, desirable, sexy as fuck wife was a damn virgin... and I was screwing her on the couch on the jet like some whore.

"Jesus. I'm so fucking sorry, Carmella. I didn't... I didn't know."

I started to withdraw, but she reached back and grabbed my ass. "No. I -- I want this. Want you."

"Honey, if I'd known, I'd have at least waited

until we were at the cabin. With a nice bed. A pretty view."

She looked at me over her shoulder, her body relaxing a little. "Casper, I just need you. I don't need all that other stuff. I was a virgin when you married me, and I've remained one... because the only man I ever wanted to claim me was my husband."

I pressed my forehead to her shoulder, trying to sort through the shit in my head. My cock jerked inside her and I decided to give us both what we needed. I started thrusting slowly, not wanting to hurt her more than I already had. The streak of blood on my cock made some possessive beast rise inside me. She was mine. *Only* mine. No one had ever fucked her but me, and that's how it would God damn remain until I drew my last breath.

"Hold on, baby. Rub your clit. I don't know how long I can last, and I want you to come."

Her hand disappeared between her legs and I felt her fingers brush against me as she flicked her fingers over her clit. I drove into her, harder and faster, going as deep as I could. Sweat coated our bodies. Her pussy clenched me tight as she came, crying out my name. It was enough to send me over the edge, and I pounded my cum into her.

Panting, I withdrew and stared as our mingled release trickled out of her and down her thighs.

Shit. I hadn't used a condom. Hadn't even thought about it.

She'd been a virgin. I didn't think the odds were good that she was on birth control. My daughter was already grown, older than Carmella, and I was a grandfather. But as I watched my seed leak from her body, I realized that the thought of Carmella swelling with my child made a warmth settle inside me.

I jerked my pants up and lifted her. I strode over to the bathroom. Setting her on the counter, I helped clean her up, then washed my dick before tucking it back into my pants. There was a slightly dazed look in her eyes that made me smile. It seemed I hadn't lost my touch. Pressing my lips to hers, I gave her a tender kiss before pulling away again.

"I hate to bring up something unsexy but necessary at a moment like this, but I'm clean so you don't have to worry about catching anything."

The light dimmed in her eyes and she dropped her gaze before nodding.

"Hey, pretty girl. I always got tested after I was with a woman."

"I understand. You didn't consider yourself truly married."

I tipped my head and fought not to smile. "Carmella."

She refused to look at me.

"Honey, I haven't been with a woman since the day I married you. I won't lie. I tried. Got her to a hotel room, watched her strip, and then... I didn't get fucking hard. All I could see were your eyes and soft smile."

"Am I supposed to be thrilled that you had a naked woman in a hotel room but couldn't get it up?"

Well, this wasn't going the way I'd anticipated. Then again, I'd never thought I'd want to keep her.

"I'm an asshole. I admit it." I rubbed a hand down my beard. "Carmella, I haven't been faithful to a woman since my late wife passed away. When she died, I vowed that I'd never love again, never get married. I broke part of that vow when I married you. Maybe part of me was trying to prove a point that night."

"What point?" she asked.

"That even though I'd married you, I wouldn't love you. I wouldn't let you get close. And I wouldn't break my vow to Isabella."

Her gaze softened a little. "You promised your daughter you'd never fall in love? Never get married?"

I nodded. "I did. And I broke that promise."

"Only part," she reminded me.

I shrugged a shoulder, then pressed a kiss to her lips. "Maybe. But, honey, I think I'm already on the way to falling for you. I don't want a divorce, Carmella. I'm keeping you."

"And the woman in the hotel that night?" she asked.

"Haven't thought of her since then. But I knew you deserved the truth, even if it didn't paint me in a favorable light. I kissed her, flirted with her... but once her clothes came off, I realized I couldn't do it. I walked out."

She looked so vulnerable sitting there. I smoothed her hair back from her face and pulled her against my chest. I just held her, hoping she'd feel how sorry I was, how much I wished I could change the past. If I could do it all over again, I'd have never left her alone all these years. I wouldn't have tried to sleep with another woman. And I damn sure wouldn't have kept her from my family.

"I'm sorry, Carmella. I'm sorry for all the pain I've caused you."

She clutched me tight and I felt the moisture of her tears soak into my shirt. Yeah, I'd been an asshole again. I doubted it would be the last time either.

"Pretty girl, do you think you can give me another chance? Let me make things right? I promise to always be faithful. I won't leave you again, not unless I intend to come back home. All this may have started with me planning to divorce you, but I don't want that anymore, Carmella. You're mine, and I'm keeping you."

She sniffled and looked up at me. "Don't I get a say in this?"

"Nope."

A slight smile graced her lips, then she hugged me again. "I guess everyone deserves a second chance, but you only get one. Screw it up, and I'll find a way to punish you."

"I can live with that."

I helped her dress, then we talked the rest of the way. By the time the jet landed, I knew that everything would be just fine between us. Now I just needed to figure out who was trying to fuck up my holiday, give my wife the best Christmas she'd ever had, and introduce her to my daughter and grandkids.

What could possibly go wrong?

Chapter Five

Carmella

Casper had shown me the cabin -- eight bedrooms! -- and let me get settled. I'd heard him on the phone in his office and tried to give him some space. I knew he was worried about the men who had broken into the other house. When we'd arrived, a tree had been propped against the cabin on the wide front porch and tons of boxes were stacked alongside it. He'd not said much about it, but right before he disappeared into his office, two men had shown up and hauled the tree inside.

Now it stood near the front window in the living room and the boxes were stacked around the space. The men had opened a few and pulled out boxes of lights and ornaments. Once they had strung the lights on the tree, I'd directed them in hanging the ornaments toward the top, then shooed them away. Decorating a tree had always been fun, even when I'd been alone and feeling a bit blue.

I turned on the TV and selected a music app, then found Christmas songs. Mrs. Weathers had always played the classics and I found that I enjoyed them as well. The last ten years hadn't been very happy ones, but Mrs. Weathers and Bowen had always tried to make the holidays magical. I hoped they were doing all right and that Casper hadn't been hard on them for keeping my secret.

I touched my head, for the first time thankful that he'd forced the surgery on me. I was fully healed now, and I'd expected him to shut me out. Instead, by some miracle, he wanted to keep me. Smiling, I hummed along with the music and decorated the tree. I hated that I didn't have a gift for Casper, but I didn't think he'd let me go shopping until the danger had passed.

Arms went around my waist and I was hauled back against a hard chest. I tipped my head back and smiled up at my husband. "Finished with work?"

"For now."

"Good news or bad news?" I asked, trying to read the expression in his eyes.

"Wire was able to get some intel together for me. It wasn't Raul Montenegro who sent those men. And he's not behind the threat I'd received in his name. In fact... he's dead."

My lips parted. "Dead?"

"Someone took him out about two years ago. There's a new man in charge of his operation."

"Is that who threatened you?"

"No. And the men who broke in weren't from him either. They were sent by..." he mumbled something I didn't quite catch.

"I'm sorry, what?"

Casper sighed and buried his face against my neck. "My family knows about you. They've always known I was married, but it seems my grandchildren thought that meant you were someone bad."

I pulled away so I could face him, feeling more and more confused.

"Casper, what do your grandkids have to do with anything?"

"My little Lyssa is nine, and normally she's the sweetest little girl. But she's best friends with Venom's two kids, Farrah and Mariah."

"Casper..."

He held up a hand. "I'm getting to it. So Lyssa told Farrah and Mariah that her grandpa was married to a bad, evil woman."

I folded my arms and arched an eyebrow in disbelief. "Are you trying to convince me your granddaughter hired killers to take me out?"

He waved a hand and started to pace.

"Casper, what the hell is going on?"

"Lyssa, Farrah, and Mariah got into Torch's computer. He usually keeps his home office locked and Wire helped him secure his computer. It seems Torch was in a hurry when Isabella got sick the other morning, and the kids got into his office and accessed his files and email."

"Um. Casper. That's completely insane. You know that, right? There's no way some little kids sent those men."

He gave a humorless laugh and pulled out his cell phone, then dialed a number and put it on speaker.

"Now what, fucker?" a gruff voice demanded.

"Torch, could you please tell my wife what you already told me? She thinks I'm making it up."

Torch growled and I heard something slamming around. "Fucking kids."

"Wait." I moved closer to the phone. "Are you telling me that it's true? Your kids tried to have me killed?"

Torch sighed and I heard what sounded like boots on a wood floor. Then the creak of a door.

"All right, brats, tell your Grandma Carmella what you did," Torch said.

Casper snickered at the name and I glared.

"We're sorry," said a contrite girl's voice. "We thought you were a bad lady. We didn't mean to hurt you, Grandma Carmella."

I was going to kill Torch for labeling me as "grandma" when I was younger than his wife. But the little girl on the phone was melting my heart.

"Sweetheart, how exactly did you send those men to the house?" I asked.

"Daddy's book just said 'clean-up crew' so we thought they would make you not bad anymore," said Lyssa.

"Carmella was never bad," Casper said. "You know what you did was incredibly wrong, right?"

"*They* were wrong?" Torch asked. "Care to tell them what happened when those men broke into your house? For that matter, you owe me for them going out there to begin with. They took that shit out of the balance I keep with their company; you know for when I actually need them."

"Shut it, old man." Casper sneered at the device in his hand. "I thought they were going to kill my wife. And no, I'm not paying for that shit! If you'd had your computer locked down, none of this would have happened."

"Grandpa, I'm really sorry," Lyssa said. "Daddy said Santa is going to bring me coal now, and I really wanted some video games."

"I think you've had enough time with electronic devices," Torch said. "We'll discuss this more later. I'm very disappointed with you."

I heard the door close and Torch sighed.

"So your kid really did send those men? How? I mean... I guess you explained how, but this all seems to..."

Torch snorted and Casper did as well at the same time.

"I think your daughter frightens me," I said.

"That's nothing. You should meet Havoc and Jordan's little demon spawn. Now that kid is going to be trouble. Hell, maybe she'll take over Casper's job when he retires."

"I -- I -- I…" I sank onto the sofa and just stared. What the hell kinds of kids were these? Maybe I should rethink the whole marriage to Casper thing. If he came as a package deal with kids who could send killers after someone, I wasn't sure I wanted to be part of the family after all.

"I think we broke her. I'll call you later. And make sure that shit with those men is handled. I don't want anyone knocking on my door because I protected my wife just because you can't control your family," Casper said, then hung up the call.

He hunkered in front of me, reaching for my hands. I felt… I didn't know what the hell I felt. Kids had tried to have me killed. Kids. Had. Tried. To. Kill. Me. I couldn't quite process what sorts of evil little demons would do such a thing. Even living in the shadow of my father, I'd never experienced anything like this. Maybe I didn't want to meet them, or their parents.

"Honey, look at me."

I looked up, obeying the command in his tone.

"The girls have never done anything like this before, and I can promise they never will again. Not only is Torch livid, but I heard Venom is on the warpath too. Those girls are going to be on lockdown so tight, they won't be able to date or socialize with anyone their age until they're ninety."

I bit my lip so I wouldn't smile.

"It's okay. You can laugh. When I finished staring at the message on my phone in shock and confusion, then went through pure rage, I settled on laughter. It's not like I'm going to string up my own granddaughter."

"I don't know, Casper. If your family is a package deal, I may want that divorce after all."

He glowered at me and I couldn't hold back the giggle that rose in my throat.

"Get up, woman. We have a house to decorate, unless you want me to hire someone? Now that I know there isn't any danger, we don't have to stay locked up, but I'm not ready to leave either."

"Don't you always spend the holidays with your family?"

He took my hand, pulled me close, and kissed me. "I am. You're my family too, Carmella."

I went back to decorating the tree while he started a fire in the massive stone fireplace. It took hours to get all the ornaments up and trim the mantle with holly and stockings. I collapsed onto the rug in the front of the fire and Casper came down next to me, two mugs in his hands. I'd never met anyone who could sit without having to brace themselves, at least no one his age. He might not look like he was old enough to be my dad, but I knew he was in his fifties now.

He handed a mug to me and I smiled at the marshmallows floating on top. Hot cocoa! My favorite holiday treat. Well, okay, *one* of my favorite holiday treats. I didn't know how he'd guessed, or if he'd spoken to Mrs. Weathers. I missed her! She'd been my friend, but she was also the closest thing I'd had to a mother in a long while.

"Why haven't you aged?" I asked. "And why is your hair lighter? It was nearly black before."

He ran a hand down his beard. "I've never told you what I do for a living, and I never will. Let's just say that it's in my best interest, and those who are close to me, if I change my appearance a little here and there. Not enough that I'm completely different, but take off some years and it makes people second-guess themselves. Maybe I'm the man they're looking for, or maybe I'm just someone who bears an uncanny resemblance."

"So one day you'll look younger than me?"

He gave a bark of laughter. "I don't think there's enough plastic surgery in the world to make that happen. Honestly, I think I'm about done putting my life on the line. The money was nice, but I have enough I don't really need more. What would you think about being married to an old man who *looks* like an old man?"

I ran my fingers through his hair. "I kind of like this color on you, but I don't think plastic surgery is necessary."

"Then I'll keep the color a while." He kissed me. "Anything for my wife."

"Anything?" I asked.

He set his mug aside and leaned in closer. "What does my sexy little wife want?"

"The tree is lit. The fireplace is going. Snow is falling outside. We're in a cabin, alone, Casper. Can you think of a more romantic setting?"

"Stay right here."

He got up and walked out of the room, only to return a few minutes later with an armful of blankets. He gave me a chin nudge to get up, so I scurried out of the way. Casper spread a thick comforter over the rug, then dropped the other on top. When he reached for the button on his shirt and started unfastening it, I quickly shimmied out of my clothes. I was still tender between my legs, but I wanted him again.

Casper knelt on the blanket and pulled me down. He covered my body with his before kissing me deeply. Feeling every hard inch of him against me, made me shiver in the best of ways. I'd always wanted this! Wanted him... He'd made me his wife in truth, showed me what real passion felt like.

His lips skimmed my collarbone, then he rubbed his beard against my nipples, first one, then the other. I wrapped my legs around him, wanting to beg him to take me already. But Casper didn't seem to be in a rush. He nipped, licked, and sucked on my nipples, making me ache. I scored my nails down his back, and Casper growled before kissing me again.

"I want to go slow. Make you beg and scream," he said.

"I don't need slow."

"Good." He thrust into me, and my back arched as pleasure zinged along my nerve endings. "Because I don't think I'm capable of it."

He gripped my ass as he drove into me. Casper held my gaze as he claimed me, his cock stretching and filling me with every stroke. He twisted his hips a little on the next plunge of his cock, pressing against my clit, and I saw stars.

"Oh, God!"

Casper kissed me, his lips devouring mine as he fucked me harder. I started coming, screaming as ecstasy poured through me, leaving me in a boneless puddle. Still he didn't stop.

"Tug on your nipples, Carmella. Come again."

I whimpered as I cupped my breasts and lightly tweaked the hard peaks. He growled a warning, his eyes burning bright, and I pinched and pulled harder on them. Satisfaction gleamed in his eyes as my pussy tightened on him.

"Twist them."

I did as he commanded and came even harder than before. The world was still spinning when I felt the hot spurts of his release inside me. Casper grunted with every stroke until he stilled, his cock pulsing deep in my pussy.

"Damn, honey. You make me feel thirty instead of…"

I placed a finger over his lips. "Age is just a number, Casper. And there are far more important things to count."

"Like what?"

"Orgasms?"

Casper burst out laughing, then pulled free of my body. My eyes went a little wide when I realized he was still hard. I'd felt him come, and the proof slipping from my body even now.

"Turn over. Let's see if we can add a few more of those to our day."

I scrambled to turn over and get on my hands and knees, but it must not have been quite how he wanted me. Casper pushed at the center of my back until I pressed my breasts to the blanket and stuck my ass farther in the air. He nudged my legs apart more, then made me yelp when he bit my ass cheek.

His body came over mine, his nose tracing a line along my shoulder. "How hard and deep can you take me, baby girl? How rough is too rough?"

My heart started to race, and my pussy throbbed in anticipation. Even if I hadn't had sex before Casper, I'd read plenty of romances. The naughtier the better.

"I'll take whatever you give me," I said boldly, then hoped I wasn't lying.

"Really?"

I nodded.

"And if I wanted to shove my cock up your ass?"

My breath stalled in my lungs, then I felt him chuckle.

"The look on your face! I'm messing with you,

honey. Not my thing." He nipped my shoulder. "But I'm going to pound this pussy so damn hard. You're going to be thoroughly fucked before we're done today."

"Casper." His name came out more of a sigh. "Please."

"I think we need to open an early Christmas present. Don't you?"

Wait. What? He wanted to stop and open presents? Now? He pulled open a box and I heard some packaging ripping apart. Next thing I knew, he was blindfolding me, then reaching for my hands.

"Give me your wrists, baby."

I put them behind my back and felt cool leather as he buckled cuffs around my wrists. Then I heard a whirring sound and nearly came just from the thought of what he might do to me next.

"I won't put my cock anywhere uncomfortable, but I think you might like what I have planned for you. Trust me?"

"Yes." And I did. Maybe I shouldn't have, but deep down, I knew he'd never do something to hurt me. He'd injured my feelings before, but he'd always made sure I had everything I needed.

I shrieked when he placed a vibrator against my clit, rubbing in small circles that had me coming in seconds. Except I didn't stop. I came and came... it was like a never-ending orgasm. When I thought I couldn't take any more, he plunged it into my pussy, stroking it in and out before teasing my clit again.

"Casper. I can't..."

"You can and you will. You'll take anything I give you, right?"

I whimpered and nodded.

I heard the click of something, then a cold

wetness slid down the crack of my ass, then more liquid.

"Casper! What are you…"

His hand cracked down my ass cheek. "Quiet, girl. Just lie there and enjoy. If you don't like it, just say so."

I couldn't say I didn't like it because so far, I did. A lot. I'd never realized Casper had a kinky side. Or maybe this was just normal sex to most people. I didn't really have anything to base the experience off of except books. And who knew if anything in those stories was true or even possible.

He rubbed the vibrator over my clit again until another orgasm ripped through me, then he started working the toy into my ass. I sucked in a breath, about to tell him I didn't like it, when he filled my pussy with his cock. The double penetration felt strange, and pinched, and yet… The vibrations of the toy, and the slide of Casper's cock, felt so damn good it was almost painful.

"Casper. Oh, God. I… I…"

"What do you want, pretty girl?"

"Fuck me! God, Casper! Just fuck me."

He chuckled and started thrusting, using the toy to drive my passion higher. I lost count of how many times he made me come, but I was close to tears when he buried the toy in my ass and started fucking me in earnest. He bellowed as he came, filling me up with his cum. Every inch of my body felt hypersensitive.

His cock twitched inside me. He stroked the toy in and out a few more times before withdrawing it and shutting it off.

"It seems my darling little Carmella is a dirty girl. You liked that, didn't you?"

"Y-yes."

"No worries, honey. I don't have a dungeon or anything like that. I'm not a Dom in the true sense of the word. Just like to play like this every now and then."

He pulled out and then unbuckled the leather cuffs. The blindfold was the last to go, then he pulled me against him and curled around me, holding me close.

"Anything you want or need, is yours, Carmella. All you have to do is ask. You want to play like this again, you tell me. If there's something you want to try, then we will."

I wanted to tell him all I wanted was for him to love me, but I knew it would ruin the moment. He'd admitted he might be falling for me, but that was different. The beginnings of feelings and tumbling completely over that ledge were two different ends of the spectrum.

"We'll get some rest, then figure out what's in the kitchen for dinner." He kissed my shoulder. "Thank you."

"For what?" I asked, sleep already pulling at me.

"For giving me another chance."

I smiled and then drifted off, dreaming of Casper and the love I worried I'd never experience.

Chapter Six

Casper
Christmas Eve Night

I'd always spent the holidays with my daughter and grandkids. This was the first year I would miss out on watching them open presents. Part of me wanted to see them, but I was enjoying my time with Carmella. Every day I fell for her a little more. If an assassin like me had a heart, then she'd own it. I'd done a lot of bad shit in my life. Killed without mercy.

Maybe having Carmella would soften those edges. Already she made me want to be a better man. I hadn't told her, but I'd been doing my damnedest to knock her up. I hadn't used protection any of the times I'd fucked her, and I'd bent her over or wrapped her legs around my waist every time I'd gotten hard. For someone my age, I'd been impressed with my ability to keep up with her. My dick seemed to think we were twenty years younger.

We'd christened the kitchen counters, the table, the dryer, every chair and couch in the house, our bed, the rug in front of the fireplace, and just about every flat fucking surface in the house. If it weren't snowing outside and cold as fuck, I'd have taken her out there too. Carmella was bent over in front of the tree, rearranging the presents. The Christmas-themed dress she had on was cute as well, and oh so easy to flip up so I could shove her panties aside and slide in deep.

I crossed the room and leaned over her, brushing my lips against her neck as I inched up her skirt. She giggled and her gaze caught mine.

"You're insatiable."

"Complaining?"

She shook her head, a smile on her lips.

Working my belt loose and pulling down my zipper, I freed my cock. Her panties were damp, but it seemed like she stayed wet. Lucky me! I moved them to the side and rubbed my cock against her pussy. Christ! So fucking slick and ready! I notched my cock at her entrance and shoved in deep, groaning at how tight she was.

"God, baby. You feel so fucking amazing."

"Casper! Please!"

I wrapped an arm around her waist to hold her up as I started thrusting. I rubbed her clit, needing her to come fast because I was already too fucking close. I pinched the little bud and she bucked in my arms, flooding me with her release. I pounded into her, not stopping until I unloaded, every drip of my cum shooting into her.

Pulling free, I admired the view a moment, then let her panties cover her pussy again. Her skirt dropped back over her ass and I tucked myself away before fastening my pants and belt. Carmella turned and flung her arms around my neck, kissing me long and deep.

"Merry Christmas, Carmella."

"Christmas is tomorrow," she reminded me with a smile.

"Maybe, but looks like I got my gift early."

"Me or sex?"

I smirked. "Both. Although I plan on lots more of that second one. If you're sore, better plan on a hot soak in a little bit."

She sighed and leaned against me, pressing her cheek to my chest.

I was tempted to carry her upstairs when I heard the front door open and what sounded like a herd of buffalo come racing toward the living room. I tensed, not sure what to expect, but it sure as fuck hadn't been my three grandkids. Lyssa led the pack with her younger siblings, Portia and Hadrian, bringing up the rear. Then my heavily pregnant daughter and her husband Torch came in.

"What the fuck, Isabella? You aren't supposed to travel!" I withdrew from Carmella to give my daughter a piece of my mind. "Are you trying to go into labor early?"

"Relax, Daddy. I checked with the doctor. He wasn't thrilled, but I told him I wouldn't miss Christmas with you. He made Torch stop every two hours to give me a half-hour break, and it took us several days to get here. I'm fine." Isabella hugged me, then pulled back, her nose wrinkled in disgust. "Oh, my God! Tell me you didn't just…"

She made a gagging noise, then rushed from the room with Torch chuckling and trailing after her.

Well, that had certainly never happened before. I rubbed the back of my neck.

"Grandpa, is this our Grandma Carmella?" asked Lyssa. "She looks younger than Mommy."

Fuck my life.

"That's because I am younger than your mommy," Carmella said, leaning down to stare at the pint-sized terror. "If you want, you can just call me Carmella. You don't have to call me grandma."

Lyssa swung her gaze to me, then back to Carmella. "But you're married to Grandpa, right?"

Carmella nodded.

"Then you're our grandma," said Portia. "I'm Portia and I think you're pretty."

Carmella smiled widely. "I think you're pretty too, and so is your sister. Who is the handsome young man with you?"

"That's Hadrian," I said.

Portia, Lyssa, and Hadrian all stared at her.

"Are you going to have more kids since our mom is too old to be your daughter?" Lyssa asked.

Carmella opened and shut her mouth a few times.

"Yes, we are. As soon as possible," I said.

Carmella froze, then slowly turned to look at me. Her eyes flashed, and then her mouth dropped open again. "You! You've been trying to get me pregnant on purpose!"

I shrugged a shoulder. "Guilty. And I'd planned to try several more times tonight before our unexpected guests arrived."

I heard a gagging noise again and turned to see Isabella had returned. Torch held her arm to keep her from running. She might as well get used to it. Carmella was here to stay. I wouldn't keep her separate from the family anymore. She deserved better. She deserved… everything.

"Grandpa, will Santa find us here tomorrow?" Portia asked.

"Absolutely," Carmella answered. "I happen to know that Santa is pure magic, and he knows where you are all the time, and if you're being naughty or nice."

Lyssa's eyes rounded. "Oh, no. I was very, very bad. Is Santa going to give me coal since I sent those men to clean you?"

Carmella rolled her lips in and I knew she was trying not to laugh.

"I'm sure Santa understands it was a mistake. But you may need to be extra good all the way until next Christmas to make up for it," I said.

Lyssa nodded her head so hard I thought it

might fall off.

"All right, kids. Give your Grandpa and Grandma some space. I'll carry our bags upstairs. The three of you can share a room right next to me and your mom so you don't get into mischief. No sneaking downstairs in the middle of the night, or leaving your room at all," Torch said.

As the kids marched out of the room, my daughter lingered a moment and came closer. She kept looking at Carmella, but I couldn't tell what she was thinking. Usually, Isabella was an open book, but the one time I needed to know her thoughts, they eluded me. She kept a blank look on her face and stopped in front of my wife.

"My father promised me he'd never marry, never love anyone again after my mother died. She was his one and only."

Carmella swallowed audibly, tears misting her eyes as she nodded. "I know. And he won't break at least part of that promise. He didn't have a choice but to marry me, but your mother will always be the woman he loves."

It felt like ice water doused me from head to toe.

"Isabella, I need you to leave the room a minute."

She nodded and walked out.

I faced Carmella and watched as the tears leaked from the corners of her eyes and down her cheeks. She hastily wiped at them, but more followed. I'd done this. Broken her.

I reached out and tugged her closer, wrapping my arms around her.

"Carmella, I know what I said before, and at the time it was true. I did make that vow to Isabella. I'd had every intention of keeping it." She sniffled and tried to pull away, but I wouldn't let her. "Then I got to know the stunning woman I'd married. Yes, I've been trying to knock you up on purpose. I want to see you swollen with my child, hold your hand as you give birth, and watch our son or daughter suckle at your breast. I want a life with you, Carmella. A real marriage, with laughter, kids... everything. Even love."

She looked at me, waiting patiently for me to say the words she needed so desperately.

"I love you, Carmella. I didn't want to, didn't plan for it, but it happened. I've fallen for you, and I want to spend the rest of my life by your side."

"I love you too, Casper, but... are you sure?"

I wiped her tears and kissed her. "I'm sure."

Lifting her into my arms, I carried her upstairs and down the hall to our room. I could hear the grandkids squealing in the bedroom as far down the hall from the master suite as possible, and I was grateful Torch had done that.

I shut and locked the door and didn't stop until I'd reached the bathroom. I set Carmella on the counter and started the shower, then stripped out of my clothes and pulled off hers as well. This time it wasn't about sex, or making a baby. She needed comfort, needed to know that she was loved, and I was going to prove it.

I stepped into the shower and pulled her in behind me, then shut the door. I spent the next twenty minutes, washing her, touching her, and trying to convey everything I felt without words. She clung to me as the soap swirled down the drain, and I was sorry that I'd taken so long to go to her. We could have spent the last decade together, already had kids. All because I'd been determined to keep a vow I should have never made.

"I love you, honey. I'm sorry it took me so long

to come for you."

She went up on her tiptoes and kissed me, but I set her back.

"That's not why I brought you in here. No sex. Not right now anyway. Later on you can show me just how naughty you are."

She playfully smacked my chest.

"Maybe you can dress up as my sexy elf while I play Santa tonight."

"Oh really?" she asked.

"Mmm. If you're really lucky, I'll let you lick my candy cane. Give you the North Pole special."

It only took her a moment to burst out laughing. "Oh my God. That was so cheesy."

Seeing her laugh, true happiness etched on her face, was the best Christmas present I could ever ask for. I wanted her to always feel like she did right at this moment. The presents for her under the tree were just objects. But this... the moments we'd shared, the closeness we'd discovered, that was the true gift this Christmas season.

"Come on, my sexy elf. Let's get dressed and go play Santa."

I shut off the water and helped her dry, then dried myself. I hadn't been kidding about the Santa and elf part. I really did have a Santa suit, and since I'd originally planned to go to the Dixie Reapers like I did every year, it was packed with my stuff. I'd also ordered an elf costume for Carmella, but it was for no one's eyes but mine.

When she opened the bag I set on the bed, her gaze lifted to mine, full of heat and longing. She pulled the scrap of material from the box and shimmied into it. The microfiber faux-velvet cupped her breasts and the fur trim accented the plump mounds. What was left draped over her frame and stopped just below her ass. If she bent over -- which I fully intended for her to do when we were done -- I'd get to see paradise.

"Casper, there's no bottoms."

I waggled my eyebrows. "I know."

I put on the Santa suit, complete with hat, then took her hand and dragged her from the room. The hall was quiet and I hoped the munchkins were asleep. Either way, with Torch laying down the law that they shouldn't come out of their room, I knew they'd stay put.

We crept downstairs and I hauled a box out of the closet. I'd meant for the gifts to be delivered to the Reapers compound, but somehow they had arrived here with the packages I'd bought for Carmella. She'd insisted I take her into town so she could shop for presents for me, even though I'd assured her I didn't need any. So I'd sipped coffee at the corner café on the main strip and given her two grand in cash.

As Carmella and I scattered the Santa gifts around the tree, I realized that this was my future. I'd get to spend every Christmas this way until the day I died, and I couldn't have been happier about it. I put the last gift down, then dragged my wife to the doorway and looked up at the mistletoe hanging there.

"So, Miss Elf, have you been naughty or nice? Do you get a kiss, or does Santa need to put you over his knee and spank you?"

Her lips parted and her eyes darkened.

I hauled her against me and smashed my lips to hers, gripping her bare ass with both hands. Her legs came around my waist and I backed her against the smooth doorframe. My fingers brushed over her slick pussy and I knew I needed her. Here and now.

I loosened my pants but before I could get inside

her she broke the kiss.

"Casper. Stop."

I froze. Was I hurting her?

She pointed across the room. "Chair."

I carried her across the room, then she squirmed to get down. Before I could ask what she was doing, she bent over the arm of the chair and gripped the other side. I shoved her dress up to the middle of her back and nudged her feet farther apart.

"Spank me, Santa." Carmella gave me a seductive smile over her shoulder. "I've been a naughty elf and need to be punished."

"Oh, yeah." I ran my fingers down her ass. "Just how bad have you been?"

Merriment twinkled in her eyes. "When I said I had to use the bathroom earlier, I lied. I went in there and got myself off."

I growled and smacked her ass hard enough it left a pink handprint on her cheek. She gasped and arched her back, making her ass stick out more.

Smack.

Smack.

Smack.

"Yes, Santa!"

I spanked her twice more, then shoved my cock hard and deep into her wet pussy. I'd wanted to make love to her, spend the night showering her with affection, but that wasn't what she was going to get right now. No. This was hard. Rough. And just what we both seemed to need.

"Fuck me, Casper! Don't hold back."

I growled, gripped her hips tighter, and gave her everything I had. I roared out my release the same time she came, screaming my name. Thank fuck the cabin was four thousand square feet. Maybe the kids hadn't heard their grandpa coming inside their grandma.

"Jesus, woman. You're going to kill me."

I pulled out and she turned, her dress dropping down again. She pressed her lips to mine and cuddled against me.

"Now that Santa has punished his naughty elf, maybe we can go upstairs and I can show you just how nice I can be."

I smacked her on her ass and led the way upstairs, one hand gripping my pants. "I don't think you're naughty or nice. You're a combination of the two that I can't seem to get enough of. Love you, Carmella."

"Love you too, Casper."

After I locked our door, I held her close. "You're the best present I've ever gotten."

She reached and grabbed my cock, which I hadn't bothered to tuck back into the Santa suit. Good thing the kids had stayed put! Her hand stroked up and down while she bit her lip. "Know the best part? I'm the gift that keeps on giving. You seem up for another round. Still want me to lick your candy cane... Santa?"

I smiled as she sank to her knees at my feet, and knew this would be the best fucking Christmas I'd ever had.

Epilogue

Carmella
Christmas Day

I'd woken early to make the French toast casserole Mrs. Weathers had taught me to bake a few years ago, as well as another breakfast casserole with diced ham, eggs, cheese, and hash browns. I didn't know if anyone had a food allergy, or if they'd even like what I'd made. Casper had been sleeping soundly when I'd woken early this morning, so I'd left him to rest and decided to surprise everyone with a nice Christmas breakfast. I was a little shocked the kids hadn't come running the second the sun was up high enough to light up the house.

The kitchen was amazing with two sets of double ovens and a massive cooktop that had six burners. It was perfect for making a holiday feast, and I'd spied a turkey in the fridge earlier. After locating the proper seasonings, I'd fixed the turkey and popped it into one of the ovens, then put together a dressing with shredded chicken that was also baking. The rest could wait until closer to time to eat, but I'd wanted to get the main dishes out of the way.

I heard footsteps and turned to see Isabella, rubbing her eyes and her belly.

"Morning," I mumbled, not sure what she'd think of finding me in the kitchen. It was technically half my house as Casper's wife, but after her comments last night... I didn't know where we stood.

Isabella froze and blinked at me. "Oh, hi."

"Um, I can just..." I waved at the doorway.

"Listen. I think we got off on the wrong foot. Last night... I was trying to make a point, but things got out of hand. I didn't mean to make you cry or feel like my dad would never love you, or that I didn't want you here. Truth is, I could tell right away that my dad was happier than he's been since Mom died, and I knew it was because of you."

"And that made you mad?" I asked.

"No. I didn't get to finish what I was saying last night before Dad ran me out of the room. I was trying to say that he'd promised all those things, but I knew that it had been wrong for him to make that vow. I wanted to give you my blessing, and welcome you to the family, but I didn't get the chance."

I gave her a hesitant smile. "So, we're good? You're not upset that I'm younger than you?"

Isabella held her fingers so close together you couldn't see a space. "Just by a smidge, and no. I mean, it's a little weird, but Torch is older than my dad, so who am I to judge? Besides... I kind of owe you one after my spawn sicced those men on you."

"They're certainly something."

She snorted and went to the fridge, then pulled out the milk. Isabella had no sooner filled a glass and taken a gulp when the squeals of her kids reached my ears.

"I think it's time to move things to the living room. Then we can eat breakfast after presents. I made two casseroles."

She nodded, then looped her arm through mine and we walked into the living room together. Casper was in his plaid flannel pajama pants and a thermal shirt, and I noticed Torch was dressed in jeans and a black sweater. Isabella and the kids had on pajamas too and I wondered if I was overdressed. I looked down at the Christmas dress I'd put on this morning. It was casual, or so I'd thought until now.

"Come here, beautiful," Casper said, holding out

his hand.

I went to him and he pulled me down onto his lap. The kids ripped into their presents while the rest of us watched in amazement as the paper and ribbons flew. It was like watching a pack of Tasmanian devils open presents. When they were done and each had found a toy to occupy them, Torch got up and made a stack of gifts by each of us.

"Brought some stuff with us," he said.

I ran my finger over the top gift with my name on it and fought back tears.

"What's wrong?" Casper asked low, his voice a soft hum in my ear.

"Presents. Mrs. Weathers, Bowen, and I always exchanged a gift each, and you always sent something but... I've never had so many to open. Ever."

His arms tightened around me and he kissed the side of my neck.

I got a lambskin leather jacket in a vibrant purple from Casper, as well as diamond earrings, a Coach purse, and a spa package at a place I'd never heard of before. Knowing Casper, it was probably the best of the best, and it looked like we would be going to Colorado at some point since that was the spa's location.

Casper was still and quiet. I glanced at him and saw that he held one of the gifts I'd picked out. My heart nearly stalled as I second-guessed myself.

Casper's thumb rubbed across the bottom of the silver frame. I'd had our names and wedding date engraved at the bottom, and the only picture from our wedding was behind the glass. The only reason I even had it was thanks to the priest who had married us. His secretary had taken a picture and forwarded a few copies to the house after I'd settled into my new home.

I'd carried them with me when Casper made me leave.

"I'm sorry. Maybe I shouldn't have..." I bit my lip not sure how to fix the mess I'd made of things.

"It's perfect," he said. Then he stood and carried it over to the mantle, and placed it in the center.

Casper came back and held me, kissing my cheek, neck and then my lips. We cuddled and watched the kids play, then everyone migrated to the kitchen to eat. It was easily the best day I'd ever had, and definitely my best Christmas.

"Next year we'll have one of our own," Casper said before taking a bite of his food.

"One of what?" I asked, my brow furrowed.

"Baby." He winked. "Practice makes perfect. Isn't that what they say?"

"Casper." I cast a frantic look at the others. "Not the time or place."

He leaned in closer, his lips brushing my ear. "Then my naughty elf can show me how nice she is later... after everyone goes to bed."

My cheeks warmed but I gave him a smile. I didn't know what had changed to make this incredible man fall in love with me, but I'd never been happier.

"Merry Christmas, Santa," I whispered.

"Merry Christmas... wife."

Harley Wylde

Harley Wylde is the International Bestselling Author of the Dixie Reapers MC, Devil's Boneyard MC, and Hades Abyss MC series. When Harley's writing, her motto is the hotter the better -- off-the-charts sex, commanding men, and the women who can't deny them. If you want men who talk dirty, are sexy as hell, and take what they want, then you've come to the right place. She doesn't shy away from the dangers and nastiness in the world, bringing those realities to the pages of her books, but always gives her characters a happily-ever-after and makes sure the bad guys get what they deserve.

The times Harley isn't writing, she's thinking up naughty things to do to her husband, drinking copious amounts of Starbucks, and reading. She loves to read and devours a book a day, sometimes more. She's also fond of TV shows and movies from the 1980s, as well as paranormal shows from the 1990s to today, even though she'd much rather be reading or writing. You can find out more about Harley or enter her monthly giveaway on her website. Be sure to join her newsletter while you're there to learn more about discounts, signing events, and other goodies!

Harley at Changeling: changelingpress.com/harley-wylde-a-196

Changeling Press E-Books

More Sci-Fi, Fantasy, Paranormal, and BDSM adventures available in e-book format for immediate download at ChangelingPress.com -- Werewolves, Vampires, Dragons, Shapeshifters and more -- Erotic Tales from the edge of your imagination.

What are E-Books?

E-books, or electronic books, are books designed to be read in digital format -- on your desktop or laptop computer, notebook, tablet, Smart Phone, or any electronic e-book reader.

Where can I get Changeling Press E-Books?

Changeling Press e-books are available at ChangelingPress.com, Amazon, Apple Books, Barnes & Noble, and Kobo/Walmart.

Changeling Press, LLC

ChangelingPress.com